MW01231293

LIGHT FRACTURE

Also by Deena C. Bouknight

Broken Shells

Playing Guy

Light Fracture

The light shines in the darkness, but the darkness does not overcome it.

A historical novel by Deena C. Bouknight

Charlotte—

Enjoy the journey!

D. C. Bouknight

2021

For J. and M.

CHAPTERS

Prologue: THE ASSIGNMENT

In general, I avoid first person. The mandate, "Do not use personal pronouns in your compositions," is probably still ringing in the ears of the many high school students to whom I taught English and literature during a stint at a private school in Columbia, South Carolina. There is enough narcissism in the world right now. However, this fascinating story cannot be told without informing you of how I came to know it.

As a freelance journalist, I am assigned to report on all sorts of unusual people, places, and events. Once, in my early hungry years, I had to write a piece for a local weekly newspaper on a taxidermist. But even that intrigued me. I'm a curious sort. Journalism has actually given me license to stick my nose into others' business – to go where many are not allowed. Thus, my editor for a South Carolina magazine emailed late fall 2004 and asked that I write a piece on an aging lighthouse near Folly Beach. The small town, its residents, and random lighthouse enthusiasts and historians were attempting to save it. The timing coincided with my youngest brother, Matthew, graduating with a master's degree in criminal justice from Charleston Southern

University. I decided to arrange to see the lighthouse during the same weekend.

A local dentist bestowed the title of Folly Beach Mayor met me at the marina with his 20-foot SeaPro fully gassed. It was chilly – for coastal South Carolina – but clear. He was precise about when we should meet, "because of the tides," he explained. While he coasted under the one Folly Beach bridge, Lee Westbury Bridge, and meandered through Folly Creek, which is flanked by acres of marsh grass, he explained how the prodigious structure awed him to his core. He shared history, his involvement with Save the Light, and future plans for the once-occupied beacon. When we reached the site of the Morris Island lighthouse, I realized why my guide was strict regarding time. An expansive sandbar surrounded the looming structure, and I could already see where the tide lapped at the edges. Low tide exposed a landing pad. We had a short time frame to walk to the steps of the lighthouse, tour it, and return to the boat, he explained. Linger too long and we would be surrounded by water – the sandbar swallowed by high tide.

The mayor told me that the lighthouse was never meant to be island-less. Native Indians, and then some British who established nearby Charleston, hunted on and fished from what was then an island lush with wild things that hid and bred in marsh grass, palmetto groves, and tangles of windblown pine. Yet, man's interference in nature – the building of jetties to deepen the channel – resulted in the rapid erosion of Morris Island. By the 1960s, 421 acres of the island were under water, including the area directly around the lighthouse. Just over 100 acres of the island no longer adjoin what used to be inhabited land. After the light was extinguished and the lens moved to the South Carolina Department of Parks and Recreation as a museum piece, the Coast Guard sought to demolish the lighthouse but locals fought – and continue to fight – to save it.

The mayor shared enthusiastically historical knowledge as we walked across the sandbar, mounted the structure's precarious base, long absent of entry steps, and ascended gingerly the remnants of an intricate nine-flight iron staircase spiraling out of vision.

Because of the island's proximity, at the opening of Charleston Harbor from the Atlantic and directly across from Sullivan's Island, a makeshift apparatus was erected in 1673 to guide ships. The initial attempt was simply an iron basket pillar of tar and pitch burned on the beach. Harbor taxes paid by ships entering and leaving the channels to reach the inner harbor of Charleston paid the light keeper's wages. Different methods of lights were tried, until the Commons House of Assembly in the mid-1700s determined Charleston was thriving due mainly to exports of Carolina Gold Rice and imports of English goods that settlers could not live without, so a permanent lighthouse structure was approved for construction on what became known as Morris Island. This decision was made less than 10 years before Patriots would embark on a war for independence against King George and his loyal subjects. The lighthouse structure, described by local journalists of the time as a "strange building, not over 50 feet high and 20 feet in diameter," directed upwards of 800 ships annually to the bustling southern trade city.

The Revolutionary War hampered lighthouse use until British rule exited the area and Americans again turned Charleston into a thriving seaport. In 1800, Congress appointed $5,950, a whopping sum at the time, to build a better, taller, more advanced lighthouse. And, in 1858, the lighting apparatus was upgraded to reflect the era's innovation: a Fresnel lens. But when war visited the area again – with the first shots fired for the Civil War on Fort Sumter, literally in earshot from Morris Island – the light darkened and the lighthouse was eventually destroyed to keep it from becoming a watchtower. Movie-worthy battles ensued on the dark beaches and, years later, archeologists still unearthed and cataloged soldiers' bones.

However, during Reconstruction and the literal but sluggish rebirth of South Carolina, local authorities recognized the necessity for the light. This time, the final structure, costing close to $150,000, was completed in 1876. What stands today is – as my article would convey – 158 feet high. The base is below the surface of the ground (and water now) and is eight feet thick of concrete; the surface base diameter is 36 feet. The iron lantern at the top held a massive first-order Fresnel lens, composed of rings of glass prisms positioned above and below the lamp to bend and concentrate the light into a bright beam; it could be seen by ship captains a distance of 20 or more miles. Different kinds of oil from lard to mineral were used.

Oil and work rooms were constructed, as well as outbuildings, a three-story keeper's home, and a one-room schoolhouse. Up to three lighthouse families, a main keeper and his assistants, could live comfortably on the multi-acre island. Parents either home schooled or a teacher was rowed out from James Island on Sunday afternoon or Monday and rowed back to James Island on Friday. Life on the island was somewhat structured but also carefree as families who dwelled there enjoyed the remoteness that comes with living on land surrounded by water. Yet, they could manageably access Charleston by boat when necessary.

Although heights unnerve me, the allure of the lighthouse managed my sensibilities as I climbed higher. In many places, the railing had eroded partially or completely, so my back hugged the brick interior walls. Nothing existed as a safety feature except for the steel steps beneath my feet. The view down was like peering into an endless well. Worth the arduous climb, however, was walking out onto the open deck, which was once the lantern room. I was afforded a 360-degree birds-eye view of the vast Atlantic, emerald marshes, Charleston's steeples, and nearby sea islands. I squinted to imagine the container vessel entering the harbor was one of numerous 19th century ships seen by the lighthouse keeper. Peering over at Sullivan's Island, I remembered with repulsion an Old Slave Mart docent's revelation that sick, dead, and dying slaves, thrown overboard prior to entering the Harbor, washed up in piles along beaches. I gazed at the rows of million-dollar homes, certain their owners were unaware that foundations covered sandy graves. Still, it was a breathtaking vista, and one that had undoubtedly motivated daily keepers' steps. Since I could see for miles, including the ripples caused by a far-away sandbar, the light must certainly have been discernible by captains and crew long before faint land shadows materialized.

"It's an amazing thing," expressed the mayor/dentist. I agreed. I wanted my senses so saturated with the experience that it would never leave me. Alas, though, we could see the smallish image of his boat and the sandbar around it shrinking by the minute.

Even though my intention in writing this first-person narrative was partly to enthrall you with the interesting history of the Morris Island lighthouse, I now come to the main point. As we turned to descend, and my stomach seized at the view of the downward spiral, my guide made this comment: "Must have been so horrifying … those several seconds … as she plummeted. As narrow as the middle part of the lighthouse is," he paused, "she may have even hit the railing on the way down." When he heard no responsive utterance from me, he turned to look back. I must have been a sight because he was immediately remorseful. "Oh, gosh. I'm so sorry. I'm always thinking about her when I come up here. That was really insensitive of me. Just thinking aloud. It will be alright. Just take it slow. Step where I step."

As shaken as I was at the thought of making it down without tumbling to my own death, I could not let his comment dissipate without further probing. Investigating might distract from the fear, I thought.

"Who?" My voice trembled slightly. For the first time I realized I knew nothing about the man that I was entrusting to guide me down 140-year-old rickety steps. "Agnes. Sorry. Most around here have heard the story of Agnes. It's become a ghost tale of sorts. She was a lighthouse keeper's wife. She fell to her death after the first major shock of the earthquake. Keeper had to face some sort of tribunal for her murder but was cleared. No one really knows what happened. He and his kids just fell off the radar. Apparently, a teacher was involved, or may have seen something. No one seems to be able find any solid information."

He stopped long enough to show me a particular spot on the ledge of one of the windows where owls perch. The main door below was in view. We continued our descent. "It's all very mysterious. Some people long ago claimed to have even seen a shadow at the tower resembling the outline of a woman … behind the glass." He snickered. "Ghost stories. People do love ghost stories."

At the entrance to the lighthouse, I looked up. Then I looked at the floor and grimaced.

Lowering ourselves back down the stair-less entryway was more difficult. Plus, the sandbar just at the base had disappeared. We had to make it to a slight rock ledge and then jump a few feet to land on the firm sand. As much as half of the temporary beach was already under water. The mayor's thoughts were audible as he used channel markers to negotiate off the sandy embankment.

On the way back through the somewhat narrow passage between marshes, imaginings intruded of the lighthouse keeper, Agnes, the teacher, and the children. The mayor pointed out porpoises following in our wake and shared more history about pirates and rebel slaves, but my mind had been disturbed by his disclosure on the tower. I was in journalistic mode and vowed to discover more.

As he anchored the boat, I asked a few more closing questions about Save the Lighthouse goals, fundraising, etc. – the future of the lighthouse. Loosely planned, he told me, was a public relations scheme to briefly light up the now lens-less lighthouse using modern technology and several generators. The idea was that if enough people saw the lighthouse aglow and, simultaneously, were inundated with its history and potential demise, they would donate funds for its preservation.

I thanked the mayor, promised him a copy of the magazine, and opened the door of my car. Although I was supposed to rejoin my family for an ongoing graduation celebration, I crossed not the bridge to leave Folly but turned onto the island's main street, flanked with tacky beach shops and a few decent restaurants. I found myself driving toward the lighthouse.

Folly Beach is close to 19 square miles. It is surrounded by water on all sides, yet the great Atlantic Ocean is the main water source at its front. The other three sides are tidal creeks and brackish marsh waters. From the air it appears to be an untidy rectangle. On the west end is a state park and a view of Kiawah Island's seemingly unspoiled wilderness. The east end actually dead ends, with a sliver of honor-system pay-to-park spots near the beach. From there, one must walk or bike past an unimposing blockade and down an old abandoned road lined with dense island undergrowth, stately palms, and wild wind-crooked shrubs. The cracked asphalt and graffitied remains of the Coast Guard station's foundation are all that exists of human contact on this 80-acre plot now called Lighthouse Inlet Heritage Preserve. No dogs allowed; it is a resting and nesting place for birds and a lure for fishermen and shell collectors alike. It is also a picture-taking paradise, with the main draw the lighthouse.

At the road's end, one must plod through deep sand and climb a mild mound to view fully the lighthouse from Folly's shore. It's magnificent. How can man, with his own hands, build such an edifice? I had in the past seen the lighthouse from afar; but, having just experienced intimately its interior and pinnacle, I felt I knew it, and – at that moment – I discerned that Agnes might not ever leave my thoughts. Her plight, the keeper's guilt (or innocence), the effect on the children, and that teacher – what had she known, or seen? I would wrestle with intense interest. I could see it coming. Curiosity would bestir me to the point that hours of days and nights would be spent pouring through pages, searching, and investigating to glean insight into that time and place.

I ventured farther onto the beach. High tide was encroaching; surrounding the tower was a wavy moat. Two fins arched in the foreground and disappeared. An osprey hovered. I reflected and wondered for some minutes. Deep breath. It was time to go. I had an article to write and family to meet. I turned slightly, not wanting to leave it. Glancing once more at the lighthouse, my vision was momentarily impeded by what seemed to be sunlight reflecting off a fragment of metal at the top's lantern room. It shone, though briefly, directly on me. I would write the article, but I would write more.

I had to.

There was a story to tell.

THE LETTER

In darkness she sat by the window in her maple rocker, waiting. Remnants of a morning moon outlined two eastern-exposed peaks resembling blunted balsams. Shrouded, she rocked, quilt and bible at her lap. She anticipated in the cottage's early stillness the breaking light – a penetrating beam that crept up between the two mountains and directed its attention – only momentarily. Then it burst forth brilliance, illuminating her small cove, her home, her. The light was daily remembrance.

On cloudy, rainy, or snowy mornings, she was also in the rocker, watching as the gray veil or stark white overtook the day. It was the light day, though, that both lifted and lowered.

Light is life; light reveals.

Expected footsteps glided toward her. It was after the light that he always entered the main room, with the Franklin woodstove, braided rug, and hand-made laurel table. He bent to brush a kiss along her brow. "A word, Love?" His daily request and endearment.

The letter was her bookmark. She opened the bible to Isaiah and read words that were once a lifeline. Lately, she found herself revisiting:

Remember not the former things,
  nor consider the things of old.
Behold, I am doing a new thing;
  now it springs forth, do you not perceive it?
I will make a way in the wilderness
  and rivers in the desert.

"Ah, yes. But why this today, Love?"

"Thankful …"

"But …"

"I read the letter again yesterday."

"The lady doth thinketh too much, methinks."

She smiled. "It's 'protest'."

"Me knowseth …"

"Stop!" She tapped affectionately at his arm.

"It has been years," he said, subduing the playfulness. "Might the letter not have been written?"

"No. Of course. I would not be sitting here. You would not be quoting Shakespeare to me. The letter is ugly-beautiful. It's just the terribleness of what brought us to this place, this life. Sometimes I cannot help but feel guilt."

"What does that book ... those words ... tell us about a contrite spirit? The new thing is done. Let us not dishonor the gift – us, the joy, the children's lives, my work, the beauty of this place – with shame. Please, Love."

She reached for his hand. His patience with her. That serenity in adversity first drew her, welled admiration. Initially empathy, yes. But the weed blossomed. She witnessed Job's faithfulness – Christian's fortitude in the mire.

She felt soothed, for the time being. A fleeting thought: how some memories are so sweet; others tragic, unsettling.

"Dry today," he asserted, sliding his hand from hers. He opened the stove door and added a small log.

"Been dry. Worried?"

"Not like last year. Late summer rain should be on its way, dry again in the fall, and then the farmers say it's a vet vinter."

"Stop it!" she laughed. "You speak that way purposely, to vex me!"

"If it wasn't dry sometimes, I'd be out of job, right?" he continued. He smiled at her and turned to leave.

She smiled, too. Secretly, she loved it when his native tongue stole into his speech, endearing him to her even more. The "v's" and "w's" especially gave him away as not a generational mountaineer like others who worked the Bald.

The letter had come to her after he settled into the Wayah Bald lookout tower.

The man was fashioned for heights. Even at 57, old to some, his fit frame maneuvered the many rough-hewn stairs as hinds feet in high places, sometimes taking two at a time. The tower, cabin-like until many years after he left the world, was a solitary, open, chestnut structure situated at the highest point, with map, compass, and alidade as his inanimate companions. During especially dry times, another shared the tight six-by-nine-foot space. The lookout, in fact, did not suit his elevation needs. He spoke often of a higher, permanent stone structure on the grounds of the Bald, a treeless summit in North Carolina with views of Tennessee to the west and to the south extending into South Carolina toward Greenville. The northern vistas stretched beyond Sylva and Waynesville in the direction of Asheville. To the east, Georgia. Long before the tower was built for the white man to detect fires, Natives scouted game and observed packs of wolves – to whom the name "Wa-ya" is credited. There were plenty of large stones scattered on the peak. His ideas for a lofty stone edifice he shared with others in the lookout and those in town responsible for communicating state needs in Raleigh, but there was no money in 1916. Far across the Atlantic, journalists reported on a war. President Wilson told Americans he would keep them at home, but government funds for extras – roads, buildings, lookout towers – were sparse. Many whispers warned of inevitability. He expected his son was too old for a fight where Americans did not belong; it was his grandson he was most concerned about. Yet conscription, if it came, was not supposed to take those enrolled in a school or already well into careers. His sentiments did not support a conflict for borders against the same Huns who were once friends and distant neighbors of his parents.

He poured steaming ashen coffee into a potter's mug and heaped scrambled eggs and venison sausage from the warm stove onto a matching plate. In a few bites, the breakfast was consumed.

She watched him.

"The rest of last night's hash and some apples are in your lunch bucket."

"Pretty, *and* sweet."

"It's not like I don't prepare a meal for you every day."

"Yes, but I am the envy of the other vor ... workers," he said, catching his pronunciation.

"Go, be with your vorkers," she teased, "but come home to me safe and sound."

"Always do," he grinned and walked to where she sat. This time he kissed her lips, full and lingering. "You sit there for a few minutes and pray, 'Eyes clear as a Blue Ridge eagle. Nose keen as an Appalachian coyot. The woods aflame is your way, oh Lord ..."

"'... just keep our homes safe and secure," she finished.

Their lookout cottage rested just below the Bald, about a mile. It was relatively safe from fire, surrounded on one side by a spring-fed branch that trickled down to Laurel Creek. An outcropping of rocks to one side and sparse vegetation save for mosses and lichen afforded little tinder to fuel flames. Yet, forest fire peril – not tornadoes or lightning or earthquakes – terrified residents tucked in hills and hollers and especially farmers and town residents in the valleys beneath, places like Franklin and Murphy. Most everywhere in those mountains existed dense forests of pine and deep-rooted hardwoods and groves of sweet white and flaming azaleas, rhododendron, and mountain laurel. The lookouts knew the heliograph, with flashes of mirrored light spelling out in Morse code the where, when, and how of the fire's impending threat. Without warnings coming from the lookout, residents could become hemmed in and have no chance of escape. Fires often spread swiftly and indiscriminately, exploding trees and whirling erratically in various directions.

Stationed just outside populated areas, during especially dry times, were men in fire camps armed with Pulaski axes and other cartable tools to create lanes and breaks if fire broke out. And the camp loggers at the base of Standing Indian Mountain volunteered and pitched in when needed.

He made her proud, doing his part to save lives as he had done before. There was one life he could not save, but he had tried.

The letter was a blessing birthed out of a curse. It brought her there – to him. She fingered it and then put the letter back where it belonged, in the oyster-shell-inlaid cypress box. She closed the lid. Best not lean into one's own understanding when there was none, she thought.

It just was; it just is.

While the day's light had yet to scare away shadows from the ground around the cottage, she rocked and stared out the window and prayed – eyes open wide. Safety; her soul, their souls.

They were forgiven; she was assured. Still, the nagging. Had he done all he could? Had she?

There was a time and a place when the light shone in the darkness.

In the darkness, much was revealed.

THE LIGHT

Evalyn first saw the light from her place among rushes at the rough point of a peninsula jetting out behind where the formerly enslaved now farmed and lived freely. Samuel showed her the place when they were both children playing contentedly on James Island as if there were no cares or ills. She was 19 now and heartbroken. The solace of the sanctuary soothed her in the past, but it had been in daylight only. This time, a full late-summer moon was her guide along the path that led her there. She had only stepped into the opening of the marshy point when the light circled its way to her. The night became bright as day. The beam startled, hitting her full force. Illumination lasted but a second, and then it fleeted – seeking its intended target: a boat or ship needing guidance.

But Evalyn stood as still as the palms she passed on her journey there; she waited for the light to visit her again, and again. She wanted to be seen, exposed, significant.

Words on crumbled, tear-stained paper reverberated.

Dearest Evalyn,

May the Lord keep you always in His hand, safe and secure. It is not I who will do that. I made a promise to you to marry you and love you, but I am unable to uphold my promise as I love another and it would not be fair to either of us if I was unfaithful to you even in my mind. I believe you understand this more than you would dare express. I am forever sorry for this proclamation and for hurting you. Please forgive me."

Thomas

She had read the letter over and over. Memorized it. And even though she vowed Thomas' betrayal would not defeat her, it was the fourth line that wedged, immovable. She considered its meaning. Had assumptions pushed him away from her and toward another?

Evalyn squeezed the waded paper tighter in her fist, her fingernails pressing painfully into her palm. Circumstances as they were would not be her undoing. Her stepfather would not have his way. Her mother's voice would not ring true.

Each illumination from the brilliant beam imbued Evalyn with resolve. She stretched her right hand to the light, touching it, absorbing its energy. An observer may have shuddered at the spectral scene.

Standing alone in the light-punctuated darkness, Evalyn conceived a new plan. It did not include marriage or lechery or needlework.

She would teach.

THE TEACHER

"What does bird begin with? *Good.* Basket? *Good.* Brown? *Yes.*
Baby? *Well done.*"

Evalyn smiled at varied height children sitting upright, proud,
along a rough-hewn bench outside McLeod's cabin row. The summer's
heat was too stifling to teach inside the cabin. Whisper breezes from
surrounding waters lessened humidity as they converged at the avenue
of oaks. Resting in chair-straight laps were worn and damaged slates
leftover from northern well-meaning teachers who descended on the
South Carolina island during Reconstruction, which officially ended 10
years earlier. President Hayes appeased contentious Southern
Democrats by getting out of their business; Republicans, and the
unofficial marshal law that had prevailed since the war ended,
essentially followed him back to Washington. The South's discipline
ended. The Compromise of 1877 left behind remnants of
Reconstruction's benefits – education and jobs and political
appointments. But without accountability, Southerners settled into a
post-war oppression to keep negroes "in their place."

The curly-headed children, some light as a paper bag while others the glistening hue of a black bird's feathers, listened attentively. These were young children, and some mamas. Some older ones went to Cut Bridge School for a few hours in the morning but had to work in the fields most afternoons – *still*, even though they were no longer officially enslaved. They worked alongside parents beholden to new rules that said negro children could be schooled and adults could be paid, but "how much" was the big question. The children occupied homes built by their parents on small plots of land tightly grasped.

Evalyn, from an early age, understood what was at stake – what learning meant. To know was more freedom. To know was dangerous too, but some had the courage. A life kept from knowing was death to some. On the islands, especially after the war, the black and white boundaries frayed, so her friend was Samuel and no one thought too hard about it – at least while she was a little girl. His daddy knew her daddy on McLeod's place. Samuel desired knowledge, and she understood that about him right off. He had the Gullah wisdom, especially tenacity. But he wanted book knowledge, and to be taught something more than cotton and the gin and corn and where his place was.

Girls who grew up on the island were a rough and tumble sort, not like the Charleston prims just across the Ashley River. Evalyn and some of the white girls her age behaved when they needed to and dressed respectfully on Sundays, but they also knew how to make corn pone and ride stick horses and sing the Gullah songs:

"De ole sheep done know de road.

De ole sheep done know de road.

De ole sheep done know de road.

De young lam must fin de way.

De young lam must fin de way."

Evalyn remembered vividly, when they were both 11, discovering Samuel at the edge of one of McLeod's immense sea island cotton fields. Obscured behind a volunteer windmill palm, he sat on the ground, knees pulled up close, face buried. When she touched his shoulder, startling him, he looked up to her, tears streaming. It was then Evalyn learned his makeshift school had closed. The white teacher whom he loved had patted her pupils on their heads and raised the chins of the smallest ones and – swallowing her own tears – announced that she must move back to Boston. She would no longer be paid to teach them, and she could not afford to stay without income.

An ember extinguished.

In that moment, young Evalyn recognized clarity of purpose. She would share with Samuel everything learned at her white school. Her friend's love for learning would not die. She would also teach the other children scattered about McLeod's.

While attending school, when her teacher rattled the school bell at noon, Evalyn had raced first to her home, a modest two-story colonial frame on the sea island well across the Ashley River from the grand, steeple-defined city of Charleston. Clapboard siding covered in faded whitewash encased the box-style, low-pitch-roof home with a symmetric profile of two simple beams to the right of the front door and two to the left. The exact same number of railing posts occupied each side porch, with brick stairs at the entry.

Careful not to convey to her mother a hurried spirit, Evalyn tackled assigned daily chores: the basket of simple hems and seams, feeding chickens, ladling collected rain water around the base of a climbing rose bush, kneading the dough ball for a second rise. Then she was off – "to play with friends for a bit," which her mother allowed, never knowing or truly caring what her daughter was up to, as long as what needed doing was done.

Samuel, who had to work from first light until noonday hoeing fields or picking pounds of prickly cotton bolls, anticipated Evalyn's appearance. He wondered often if his father looked down from heaven above and marveled that his son was free to learn – and from a white female friend, no less. What Evalyn absorbed from her teacher each morning bubbled up and spilled over. Shared lessons in ciphering, grammar, history, and some Latin saturated Samuel's eager mind.

History, recent and way back, was a preferred subject between them. Talk of it dripped out over and over again in conversations. Their fathers were of the past, and speaking of them prevented their memories from dissipating as mist. Present foundations faltered, but not history.

Pre-war had been good to the Gray family. Evalyn's father was a master craftsman and boat builder. He had absorbed this trade at the insistence of his father and grandfather, staunch Scots with the mindset that precise wood craftsmanship was the only true skill a man ought to possess. Mr. Gray was first and foremost beholden to Master William Wallace McLeod of the prominent 1,700-acre plantation bearing his name. As a spry 30-year-old in 1851, with a reputation on the sea island and in town for the strength and poetry he brought to wood, Mr. Gray was immediately hired on by the new-to-the-area McLeod, a transplant from Edisto among long-established planters. When McLeod married Susan Lawton and earned a sizeable dowry, he invested $11,500 to prosper a struggling plantation that included 23 slaves, a few cabins, a dairy, and a kitchen. He completed a wife-and-family-suitable columned home by 1854, added 40 more slaves and a steam-engine cotton gin, and built slave cabins on each side of the promenade of oaks so that anyone entering the long drive might not misunderstand his wealth. McLeod's wife bore him three children in eight years before she died. He quickly married another, Harriet Frampton, who managed to provide a fourth child at the very same time war loomed in the nation.

Evalyn learned in snatches from her father's surviving contemporaries that he was not keen on slavery, but they reckoned his convictions were never shared, even minutely, with the family who afforded him a living. In contrast, McLeod kept no qualms regarding his rightful slavery practices. He took a prompt lead among the island's 21 plantations by logging 100-plus slaves just prior to the war, so he was a man who held his head up on the island and in town. McLeod needed a man like Mr. Gray to show his status – to manifest such materialistic virtues as impressive double-bead crown molding in the formal rooms and a cylindrical, tapered mahogany stair banister. He employed Mr. Gray to become custodian of the few flat-bottomed skiffs McLeod owned for visits to Charleston when there was no patience to wait on the ferry. These small boats also transported goods and guests, and Mr. Gray's purpose was to see that a few slaves maintained, polished, patched, and readied them. But because of his proficiency regarding all things wood, Mr. Gray also crafted McLeod's decorative furnishings: a dining room sideboard with a subtle pineapple motif, a four-poster bed with carved palms, beautiful turned-spindle cradles, and a sleek rocking horse. When not summoned by the cotton planter, Mr. Gray continued as a free agent to ply his expertise among other wealthy landholders, lawyers, bankers, and the like in town. McLeod's two concessions were that Mr. Gray make this statement to outside clients: "I am Master McLeod's woodworker, but I am available to you at this moment" and, that he never craft anything resembling a distinct line or image that had been carved, hewn, and polished for McLeod Plantation.

Evalyn knew that while her father was employed at McLeod, Samuel's father was enslaved there. And the enslaved people of McLeod kept mostly to the fields of European-prized sea-island cotton and to the Spanish live oak-lined avenue of white-washed one-room cabins – all of equal square footage and elevated off mossy soil by bricks made on the property. Many enslaved residents had spent their hours in the gin house emptying the required 70 to 100 pounds of daily picked cotton into the gin, which did its job purifying the soft cotton of its prickly seeds. Others packed export bundles taller than a man and the weight of at least three onto ships bound from Charleston Harbor to the Port of London. Depending on perspective, the more fortunate of the enslaved population were house servants, like Samuel's mother, their brown skin unblemished by the prickly cotton or the bruising of the gin. Most others, older children, women – with child or not – and men spent August through December among the rows, higher than a man's head and requiring reach for the white gold to make it into sacks. The negroes generally ignored Mr. Gray when he worked on the property, and he observed them apathetically as they went about their tasks. When told to do so, a few assisted him in his woodwork for McLeod. Samuel's father had been one of them.

Both Evalyn and Samuel were told stories about McLeod's bad, but also his "tinge good." Certainly, he was not considered an overly generous and compassionate man, but instead of driving his slaves beyond their means as was the common practice of some human property owners, McLeod assigned tasks to each and allowed them time to rest, to attend to gardens surrounding each cabin, to worship inside cabins only, to mend and cook; but his property could only have time to themselves *after* duties were completed on time and accurately. The sun rose and set, in fact, on the task system at McLeod's. Instead of beating them to uselessness, except in extreme cases, McLeod was known to throw more salt pork their way, which made slaves want to work harder for water to replenish their dehydrated bodies. But he never failed to allot each family a basket of corn weekly, and he sometimes allowed the kitchen and house slaves to pass out indiscriminately any leftovers from his own table. Occasionally, he even boasted to other planters his generosity in spoiling the slaves at least one day of the summer season with a few baskets of peaches. It was a treasured act surely to be stored up in heaven, he told his peers. McLeod would charge a few of his "pampered" slave women, usually light-skinned "sensible" ones from inside the home, with determining who should get the peaches and how far the fruit might stretch among the many inhabitants of his land. Children were first priority and then field and gin adults who experienced rare pleasures.

Mr. Gray's station in life was not anywhere in range of McLeod's, but he could afford peaches now and then, and he marveled at how carefully each peach was savored by the negroes – from the initial breaking of the fruit's skin that burst the ooze of juice to the sucking of the peach pit.

McLeod Plantation was not the largest of the sea islands, yet it held to a standard. Among other planter gentlemen in Charleston and the sea islands, a saying became commonplace: "He must be wealthy; he's walking in high cotton." There was no mistaking McLeod's 1,000 acres extending from the confluence of Wappoo Creek and Ashley River westward down Wappoo Creek and then south to James Island Creek, east to Charleston Harbor, and north back to the confluence of Ashley River and Wappoo Creek. It was a decent swath of James Island, and his slaves knew they had nowhere to run to freedom. Water surrounded them, and if they made it into Charleston, there was the threat of capture and tortures of the Work House; just the utterance of the place disciplined the problematic. McLeod and the other planters kept their enslaved from pushing boundaries by asserting their own Christianized philosophy: *"Serve your Master as you would Christ. The world has a natural order; some are slaves and some are masters. You are working to earn freedom in the afterlife."*

Evalyn hoped – judging by what she knew of her father's character – that there had to be times when he strode home on his plain dun Marsh Tacky mare, with the weight of his day's labor at McLeod's profound about his back and shoulders, cursing inwardly the whole business of enslaving a skin color. As accepted as the practice of slavery had been pre-war, Evalyn trusted her father did not share a tolerant viewpoint. Though to speak up ... *Never.* He was a carpenter, who needed a living.

Before Evalyn, the Grays owned the riding horse, a small garden plot, a chicken yard, and a paddock with an attached two-stall lean-to for the horse and a milk cow. They were prosperous by some standards, because of his carpentry salary and his wife's proficiency with needle and thread.

But cannon blasts and gunfire emanating from Charleston Harbor growled long and low through marshes and onto James Island one April evening in 1861. Within the year, McLeod's stately property became a field hospital for wounded Confederates, with surgeries performed in the parlor and officers inhabiting his bedrooms. McLeod, not keen on dying for his new country, was allowed to join the Charleston Light Dragoons, which was an opportunity afforded to the area's prominent men of means. These privileged few saw little to no action, other than the card games and horse races they conjured to pass the time, but were primarily escorts in stark white uniforms for the South Carolina dead brought home for burial. Each Dragoon was allowed to bring a slave to tend to his every need. The only real fear for McLeod and his compatriots was assignment to Battery Gregg on Morris Island where Union ships, anchored near the beachfront, opened fire on any Confederate horsemen suspected as couriers.

When the Union bore down on the Charleston area and the embers of a southern war for a cause diminished, a General Gist ordered James Island's evacuation and McLeod's family moved inland to Greenwood. He left a married slave couple in charge of his plantation, but they served no purpose to guard the site when Federal forces moved in to occupy and set up local headquarters on cotton fields left fallow. The tables had turned early in 1865 with whispers of "just a matter of time," and the 54th and 55th Massachusetts Volunteers marched into the depleted area – where the conflict began – and decided McLeod Plantation would be as good a place as any for a camp, until word came from Lincoln in Washington that fighting would ensue no longer.

At the start of the war, Mr. Gray was forced to place his chisel and myriad other carpentry tools neatly into his hand-carved tool chest and join the 17th Battalion of the South Carolina Cavalry (6th) because he proved adept as a horseman. Though he was not as spry and zealous a young man as so many fellow soldiers, their eyes wide with the fierceness of a trapped bobcat, he was able to carry a gun and wear a uniform to do his duty for South Carolina and the established Confederacy. Not to do so meant a judgment of treason and likely death.

He left his wife for two years, eventually joining the 5th South Carolina Cavalry Regiment to travel to Georgia and Florida before returning to McLeod Plantation, while it was a field hospital, with a bullet wound to his back. Mr. Gray convalesced, writhing in perspiring pain – wincing at the smell of bodily fluids and old blood – in the home where the wood once gleamed and pride was felt for the work accomplished there. But the Civil War had transformed McLeod into a utilitarian structure. Ambiance and décor no longer mattered.

Masses upon masses of Union and Confederate were buried near generations of deceased enslaved peoples on the acres of land surrounding McLeod's. Mr. Gray was glad, at first, that he was not one of them. When Mr. Gray could walk at a stoop, he ambled painstakingly to his weed-ridden, neglected home. His wife had taken refuge in Summerville with an aging aunt, uncle, and two cousins, who were sisters. But when his wife returned to a shard of the man she knew before the war, and McLeod's was no longer an employer and a home but the temporary headquarters of the new Freedman's Bureau, Mr. Gray entertained thoughts of solace under the ground. His pain would not subside, his urine was often pinkish-to-red, and he lacked the strength that might have allowed him to apply pressure on the plane and lathe.

Still, just one year following the war, when hordes of Northerners invaded the formerly gentile and now ravaged city and then spread like ants onto islands and along marshlands, Mr. Gray managed to impregnate his wife. Their coupling had produced two children before the war, but each did not make it past five months gestation. There was no thought or hope for a child after the war. Yet, she came. Evalyn Marie came to the beleaguered couple.

Mr. Gray secured basic carpentry work with the sharp-tongued Reconstruction masses. He crafted dinghies, with help from a few formerly enslaved men, including Haitian-native Samson, whose son, Samuel, was born the day after his own Evalyn. Yet, even if an opportunity had presented itself, his body was incapable of mustering the woodworking skills of his pre-war reputation. But he coped. And, as his wife secured work with her needle and thread, Mr. Gray enjoyed his daughter for two years before his body succumbed to ceaseless festering from lead and gun powder.

Evalyn had no recollection of her father, but his presence was everywhere in the home, barn, and chicken pen he constructed. Occasionally, she ran her hands over his toolbox. She swelled at the complexity of his only gift to her, a box crafted from local swamp cypress and inlaid with hand-selected, luminescent oyster shells. Knowing that his hands had toiled with the wood items she lived among gave her comfort.

Many children were fatherless, including Samuel. He knew little about his father, except for the circumstances surrounding his death, which were told in reverent tones by Samuel's mother and others who knew Samson. His mother and father, like many enslaved couples, had not legally married, and any semblance of friendship or intimacy was tucked in sparingly between plantation tasks and daily survival. Samson had cleaned up the foul waste of Confederate soldiers for months and months while McLeod's was a field hospital, yet he dared one day in post-war Charleston to walk on the sidewalk for a few seconds beside a lady. Two Confederate war survivors ended Samson for his indiscretion. Samuel and Evalyn were only toddlers when his father was found face down in a marsh at low tide, tiny fiddler crabs taking shelter in his torn and pluff-muddied shirt. The war was over, slavery was no more, but hearts and minds changed turtle slow.

******

Evalyn committed extra time to teach her friend because he wanted to understand a system that made no sense. Samuel thought becoming educated might redeem in some small way the waste of slavery, his father's death, and his mother's coinciding emotional demise. The Boston-based Reconstruction teacher had filled Samuel's head with should be's and could be's and he had decided he would one day attend negro-tolerant Wilberforce University in Ohio and become a

teacher and return to the South to teach as many children as possible –
black and white, if they let him – so ideas might change. When the
northern teacher shared about Frederick Douglass' life, Samuel's young
mind opened wide to possibilities outside his circumstances. It was
Samuel's hunger that impelled Evalyn. And as she matured, an innate
teaching spirit roused and took root. She had no interest in sewing, as
her mother did, but instead nursed a conviction to teach Samuel and
others as often and as much as possible. Knowledge was desired and
Evalyn intended to do her part to bestow it.

She had wanted to attend South Carolina Normal College to
obtain a teaching degree. But her mother and stepfather united against
Evalyn. Paying for college was a waste of money, even though the
college was generous with its scholarships. And teaching, they asserted,
was folly. Proficiency with needle and thread always supported. Food,
shelter, and clothing were necessities. Learning was not.

Evalyn's mother became emphatic that the only secure future
for a young woman, marriable or not, was dependent on needlework.
She needed her daughter's help to fulfill a steady demand by the
island's main store, Mac's Mercantile, for handsewn dresses, blouses,
aprons, and more. And, while James Island neighbors had little need

for finery, such as lace trimmings, embroidery, and brocades, northern invaders took a liking to them and Evalyn's mother did not disappoint.

Evalyn yielded to her mother's mandates, but only outwardly. One concession was that Evalyn be allowed to keep a portion of monies earned sewing specific pieces. She let her mother think she was saving the allotment for a dowry, but she hid some of the earnings behind a loose wall board in her room, and with the remaining monies she ordered and purchased instructional books through a Charleston bookseller. Evalyn told her mother they were novels, and the guise was never questioned. Her mother paid no attention to what Evalyn did by candlelight in her room in the evenings, as long as the day's sewing was accomplished.

Evalyn was so certain that God gifted her with a natural penchant to teach that she practiced on sharecropper children whenever she could find the time, and she filled in academic gaps by instructing herself through reading. She might not be able to attend Normal with other aspiring teachers, but through reading she would accomplish her goal, much like Lincoln taught himself the law. She collected and learned popular teaching texts: McGuffey's *Eclectic Primer and Reader*, the new Hart *American Literature*, Potter's *Penmanship*

Explained, and Appleton's *Elementary Geography*. On her want list were books detailing American and world history.

Since the jilting, which Evalyn tried to view as an unforeseen blessing, she was more determined to teach and earn her own living. She could not stay in her mother and stepfather's stifling, portentous home full time, no matter her mother's insistence.

The marriage rejection devastated and embarrassed Evalyn's mother. She blamed Evalyn for Thomas' head turning toward another. At every opportunity, possible reasons were voiced:

He must have been put off by your learned ways and obsession with filling those negroes' heads with nonsense.

He must have been exasperated by your independent spirit.

You didn't smile at him enough.

Your bun was too mussed … your hemline not securely pressed.

Samuel's name was never mentioned, but Evalyn sensed sometimes that it strained to slither across her mother's tongue. Evalyn suspected that her mother just did not want to give life to an unconscionable notion.

Instead, her mother pointed out to Evalyn every possible future suitor within the island's minimal marriage pool, and she harped increasingly on the importance of needlework.

"You'll probably never marry at this point, especially since everyone knows Thomas changed his mind about you, but at least you will have your needlework to make your living when I'm gone."

"But I want to teach, Mama."

"You will *not* teach! You *will* sew!"

"Yes," interjected Evalyn's stepfather. "You will stay home and sew as your mother has instructed. You must honor your mother, and me as your father."

He was not her father. Evalyn dreamed of heartening words from her own father. Mr. Gray must have been the antithesis of her stepfather, she imagined. Even in death, Mr. Gray continued to reap praise from locals. Yet, Evalyn heard no kind words expressed about her stepfather. On the contrary, his dealings with carpetbaggers and scallywags concerned many. Evalyn had no idea how he contributed income. But he brought home some money to her mother and aggrandized the circumstances for which he acquired payment. In her mother's eyes, the man was shrewd – no matter the details. She surmised her mother married him for security. Evalyn had never witnessed a loving gesture between them.

Though he never struck her, Evalyn failed to feel kindliness toward or reliance in the man. And when fullness came to her body, trepidation arose. Her form was unlike her mother's, who – though possessing imposing eyes and brows that drew onlookers to her face – carried plumpness in a short frame and wide hips set permanently from so much time spent sitting to sew. They shared the same dark blondish, thick-soft hair piled most days in a practical high bun with escaping wisps and ringlets. But Mr. Gray had bestowed to Evalyn his lean, naturally straight build and temperate, yet composed, expression. Evalyn was neither plain nor beautiful, but she was youthful. She also had a restrained fervor, with a twinge of antagonism, and so her stepfather's voice lowered to a husky rasp when he found her alone. His gaze lingered longer: while she rocked and sewed in the evenings, when she set the table for dinner, as she swept the front porch. Her mother seemed oblivious – distracted with talk, or work, or cooking. But Evalyn instinctively sensed a pressing in.

When Thomas, whom she had known since childhood, began courting her, Evalyn's heart did not overflow with love for him, kind and handsome as he was. She was merely grateful for his proposal – if, for no other reason, than to deliver her from her stepfather. Marriage to Thomas would also, she hoped, shutter feelings for a man she would never have.

Evalyn harbored no bitterness for Thomas' hand seeking another's – the lovely daughter of a grain supplier, new to the lowcountry. Evalyn had some understanding of a heart choosing involuntarily. Still, the marriage dismissal was an unexpected shroud. Evalyn had wept and prayed for her future, until the lighthouse light stirred clarity.

She must not stay in her home. The mindless needle and thread would take her soul. Her stepfather's impropriety would steal her spirit. She needed to make her way as a teacher, but she did not know how - until she saw the light, and it lit her path.

THE JOB

James Island showed its seasons on the marsh grasses. Wet plains extended beyond sight –rippled by breeze or wind – graduating from luminous green in summer to a flat emerald-brown in fall to resting russet from December to March. In spring, a pale olive gradually ascended from watery roots to make alive again the dormant sprigs.

The islands' cooling began in fall. Temperatures chilled uncomfortably some days and nights during winter months. Snow was extraordinary. Snow upon beaches – an unnatural sight. Evalyn had not witnessed it herself, but she heard stories of the rare phenomenon.

Evidence of fall approaching was the tapering off of summer's sultry humidity. More than spring, fall roused hope in Evalyn. And it was a clear, blue-sky day one October that she stood on the dock waiting for the ferry to deliver soft goods and threads for dress orders and heard men, who were awaiting passage over to Charleston, speaking of a new lighthouse keeper for Morris Island.

"Keeper Angus got called over to Georgetown," said one. "Heard they're in bad shape over there. Keeper drinking on the job.

Two ships almost rammed. Mayor there pitched a fit and fired the louse!"

"Who's keeping up Morris?" asked the other.

"Keeper More, but he's not keen on the full load. And that slip he had on the lower stairs didn't help none. Gimpy up and down because of that bruised ankle. Keeper O'Hagan helpin' out, but he needs to get back over to Sullivan's to get them station boys straight out there. They've been hit or miss of late. That eye needs to turn … not miss a beat. Boats gotta see to come in right."

"Guess keepin' the light's one of those wobbly sort o' jobs. I wouldn't want it. Living out there on the island and up and down all day. Don't like heights no ways. Gotta' keep fit as a fiddle and safe, else the job don't get done."

"A new keeper and his family are headin' here in December. Swedish fellow, I hear. Family kept a light called Nar, or some such. Can't tell you much about Sweden, 'cept it's over there near Europe somewheres. Guess he can speak some English 'cause I heard tell he wanted to come to America so bad he studied up on our ways. Not sure about his wife, and he's got a couple childrin'. He sent over a message to Angus that he needs a teacher for his childrin', so he must want 'em to learn English and American ways."

"Not sure where they'll find a spinster teacher around these parts willin' to teach out there. Maybe in Charleston, but that's a bit of a boat ride and ..."

"Excuse me, sirs. I seemed to have overheard you mention a need for a teacher for a new lighthouse family," inserted Evalyn.

"Yes," answered one.

"I happen to be a teacher in need of employment. Where might I apply for this position?"

******

Evalyn read the hand-written advertisement posted with one bent nail to the right of Mac's entryway door. It was written and signed by Keeper Bennett, but the list of dictated details were conveyed by someone who had considered thoroughly their expectations of a hired teacher.

NEEDED

1. Lighthouse teacher for two children: girl and boy, ages 9 and 11

2. Monday through Friday

3. Must find transport to and from Morris Island (not included in salary)

4. Room and board included

5. Teaching essentials: proper English – spoken and written, American history, world geography, literature of the British, arithmetic, natural sciences

6. In free time, must be reading the Bible or other proper books in room

7. No smoking or drinking of liquor

8. Teacher must be of good moral character, integrity, and honesty

9. Must not be engaged or married

10. Lack of decorum will result in immediate dismissal

11. Must provide teaching materials – reimbursements above salary will be paid

12. Wage: $2 per week

13. Begin January, 1886

14. Employers: Lias and Agnes Larsson

15. Serious candidates inquire in writing and post to Keeper Angus Bennett, James Island Post Office

Evalyn read the advertisement again and again. Carefully; slowly. A message written expressly for her. The lighthouse was not just illuminating her future; it summoned.

Emboldened, she entered Mac's. Behind the counter was Thomas' bride.

"May I have a scrap of paper and borrow a pencil, please?" Evalyn asked, unabashedly.

Flustered, the young woman shuffled some items and papers on the counter. She tore off a ragged edge of an invoice and wordlessly handed to Evalyn the scrap of paper and the remains of a hand-shorn pencil.

"Thank you."

Evalyn wrote carefully the details of the advertisement, making certain to spell the Larssons name correctly: with two "s's". Judging by the advertisement's diction, the children's parents were fastidious.

******

Evalyn's application letter felt to her as if it was a life or death labor. In securing this position, she could make her own way. She would not need to marry. Her standing in the community would be such that her mother and stepfather could not interfere. She might end up a spinster, but it would be a worthy cause. A happy lighthouse keeper and his family meant a well-run lighthouse – and, thus, safely delivered goods and sailors, many of whom were native sons of the islands. If she could prove herself as invaluable, her future and her freedom might be set. Yes, she must return each Friday afternoon to James Island and spend weekends at home. But if she were to become a professional teacher, she imagined relating to her mother with great confidence: "Certainly, mother, I will help you with that bit of mending … or finishing work, but I must prepare my lesson plans first."

Regarding her stepfather, she failed to know how she would divert him on weekends. She hoped he would see her differently. Leave her be.

Satisfied with the final draft of her letter, which included a list of books and materials already in her possession, she posted it and prayed. She prayed that common prayer of desperation: *Please do this and I'll serve you.* But she meant it. She was already attending church, honoring for the most part her mother (and stepfather), and thanking God at bedtime. But she envisioned life teaching on Morris Island as a more purposeful way to serve – an opportunity to weave a greater thread of meaning into all aspects of education.

She just needed the job.

She had to get the job.

THE ISLAND

Still far from the creek that housed the Morris Island dock, Evalyn made out the forms of Agnes and Erik and Elsa. On that misty, mild January morning 1886, the three stood, stiff and straight, white clothing against a white-washed home. They were barely outlined at first. Small pin prick soldiers. As the small boat drew nearer, the rigid shapes of the children became distinguishable. Erik was just a brush taller than Elsa. Their bodies, positioned in front of each of Agnes' legs, were held firmly in place with an arm draped over their shoulders and a mother's hand splayed slightly against their chests.

Evalyn had risen that morning at 5 with the first calls of Henry, their rooster. She did not remember sleeping. The new cotton calico dress of pale cream and peach, made by her hands, hung on a door casing. Another identically styled dress, but sewn with osnaburg, was already folded neatly and packed in a carpet bag, along with an apron, a shawl, and an extra set of undergarments. Taking up the most room in an extra bag were schoolbooks and supplies. She washed her face and dressed. Groaning, she dragged the bags to the front door and left them on the porch. She refused stubbornly any assistance from her stepfather. Since receiving the employment letter that outlined particulars regarding start date and additional expectations, a fiery resolve flared in Evalyn. Trepidation dissipated whenever she was in her stepfather's presence. Her glower seemed to deflate his dreadful attentions. And congratulatory expressions from James Islanders substantiated her new position.

Evalyn's mother, stone-faced, had refused that early morning to turn away from a crude wire mannequin form on which she was pinning a dress hem. "I'll return early Friday evening," affirmed Evalyn. There was no response. Not even a bothered sigh. Evalyn knew her mother felt abandoned by an ungrateful daughter unwilling to embrace a livelihood already established. Her mother, not an educated woman herself, considered monies spent hiring a teacher as extreme folly. She had already voiced her disregard for the Swedish Larsson family and their wasteful ways. "That mother can teach those children herself," she had said when Evalyn shared the news of her employment letter. "What do they need education for anyway? The boy will most likely become a keeper himself, and the girl will marry or she can sew or cook. You will regret this choice. This is foolishness!"

No one waved Evalyn off as Toasty, an islander whose burnt and leathery skin earned him a nickname he accepted with indifference, picked up her and the heavy-laden bags in his mule-drawn cart to make the trek down the long dirt road to Folly Creek dock. There, a negro skiff captain waited to navigate winding water paths clearly marked with tall marsh grass. She explained to both men that a few coins could be relied on twice weekly if they proved consistent in providing passage to and from her new place of employment.

Other than snowy egrets with waving feathered crowns on the hunt for marsh fish and marine worms, and low flying terns skimming the water for a quick catch, Evalyn saw nothing but winter brown tidal plains in all directions. She sat on the boat's bench, shawl grasped tightly at the neck, entranced at the paddle's disappearance and re-emergence from a glassy facade. Drips caused restrained ripples. Steadily, the lighthouse grew. Visible only above its third black stripe, it protruded above the small island's dense forest like a foreign friend. It seemed to Evalyn that the lighthouse was both at odds and at one with the forest. The lighthouse and the trees served different purposes – but both essential.

On their short journey, the small skiff maneuvered around partially sunken boats protruding from grasses and water. The previous fall's cyclone resigned them to a muddy, oyster-shell grave. *A full waste*, mumbled her companion. There were no resources to resurrect the boats. The fishermen who owned them simply had to find or buy lumber to build another. These boats lacked the importance of immersed contents such as those on the USS Keokuk, a Federal ironclad that went down just off the southern end of Morris Island during the war. The Union crew escaped. But needing the cannons that were known to be 18-feet below the surface, hand-picked stealth Confederates – working secretly at night – used applied physics to concoct a plan to raise the behemoth weapons. Each heroic diver, all locals, filled lungs, submerged, turned a screw holding each cannon, and surfaced, again and again and again. Once freed from their watery bondage, the two cannons were raised by way of a crank-and-hoist scheme involving 1,500 sandbags to counter-balance weight. Even though fairly recent history, the tale was legend on the islands and in Charleston because of the magnitude of the feat. Despite losing the war, the men's bravery, aptitude, and strength was proof to many Southerners of Confederate ingenuity and tenacity. Evalyn's mind lingered on the details; she decided her new charges would learn this bit of local history and more. And, since the Larssons hailed from a country far from her own still-healing one, Evalyn would feel no betrayal in teaching the children all angles of the dreaded war, good and bad and South and North.

Home seemed an ocean versus a tidal creek away as the boat glided toward the small welcoming party. The husband/father was unseen; most likely he was at work in the lighthouse, which seemed to Evalyn, now that she was close to it, like an erect, striped sentry donning a pointy black cap. The tower loomed at the ready, two windows and its doorway facing south, from whence she had come. She surmised that at least for the sake of symmetry two more windows must face north – in the direction of Sullivan's Island and Fort Moultrie. She learned later she was right. Though she could not see them for the island's trees, Charleston and its steeples were to the west; to the east, nothing but an immeasurable watery horizon.

The house, which came fully into view as the boat rounded the last curve in the marsh road, looked inviting and adequate, but reality suddenly bore down on Evalyn. When the boat unburdened her, plus her personal articles and school supplies, she would be alone and isolated for a week with strangers. Trepidation gripped her, but only momentarily. Smiling and a light heart were rebukes to the devil, Samuel always told her. Singing, too. Old slave practices kept hopelessness at bay.

She wished she could have spoken to him about her teaching job. He was a comfort, a confidant, even though he was not supposed to be. The fleeting thought of him, his model of strength and calm, slowed her jittery heart. She allowed herself a few seconds to think on him. Samuel had figured out he could earn more money mining for phosphate along the Ashley River than if he toiled in fields. Samuel was saving for a northern education. For his future goals he was called "uppity" by some of his kin and other now-free women and men who chose to stay on at McLeod's after young William II decided to try mustering a livelihood out of an unrecognizable landscape. But Samuel paid no attention to naysayers. "Better the mines than the fields," Samuel told Evalyn, "and they'll eat every last word when I come back with the first college degree any of 'em ever seen." She smiled, envisioning Samuel's wide, confident grin.

Evalyn contemplated the irony of the senior McLeod's demise. As the war ended, he had made it almost to Monck's Corner, just 37 miles from his beloved home, when his horse died and he was forced to walk. Exhausted and ill with pneumonia, William senior died and was buried in an unmarked grave. Though the war had mostly ravished James Island, 15-year-old "Willie" returned with his two younger sisters to start afresh. To get his father's plantation back in McLeod hands, Willie had to endure the recitation of an oath of allegiance to the United States of America and agree to treat his family's formerly enslaved persons with dignity and respect.

Evalyn recognized that while Samuel and his friends and family were free and in familiar surroundings, they were all attempting a new way of life unknown in the South. Freedom meant possibilities, but struggles still. Evalyn identified – somewhat.

Here she was, jilted and fatherless, but with a chance to narrate a new life, an important one that may make a marked difference in the lives of at least two children. The lighthouse before her was a tangible symbol of her new employment, and viewing it up close made her feel both exhilarated and troubled. But she steeled herself not to be afraid of her future.

The woman Evalyn knew only by the details of an advertisement pressed her son forward as the boat was tied dock. "Miss Gray," said Erik, a friendly smile creasing his cheeks. "Velcome." He pointed to himself: "Erik." And then he held up nine fingers and said, "Nine." He pointed to the bags. "Yes? Carry?"

"Certainly. Thank you, sir. You are most polite." She glanced up to make approving eye contact with Agnes and shrunk slightly at her stern expression. Evalyn straightened her skirt and reached back to check for stray hairs before approaching mother and daughter. Elsa curtsied but did not smile. "Elsa." She held up seven fingers.

"Seven!" asserted Agnes, who curtsied expressionless and then grabbed her daughter's hand and turned to lead the party up a long plank walkway toward the house. The skiff captain followed with the heaviest bag of books. But a few yards from the entryway, Agnes turned abruptly and motioned for the man to set the books down onto the walkway. He looked confusedly at Evalyn, who nodded her head. Agnes gestured for him to return back to the boat as if she were shooing a feral dog.

"Thank you! Please return on Friday afternoon!" Evalyn called after him. He raised his hand without turning back.

Evalyn had little time to consider the feelings of the man who ought her to the island. Agnes marched toward the home's entrance and Evalyn felt engulfed by the lighthouse's enormity compared to even the substantial size of the home, with its two chimneys, pitched roofs, and slight Victorian features. Perfectly symmetrical architecturally, the storied home offered two entryway porches balancing its southside view. An ornamental metal gate hung between finial-topped columns attached in both directions to a decorative concrete fence. An urge seized her to drop her bags and walk not inside the home, but around and behind it and straight into the lighthouse. Fleetingly, she imagined her flat hand against the cool, hard walls and the apprehension and elation of climbing to the top.

"Here, Miss!"

Agnes' command jolted Evalyn to her new reality.

"You come here." Agnes motioned her through the entryway parlor, sparsely proportioned, but beautiful nonetheless, to the wide polished staircase.

Evalyn ascended dutifully the three flights of stairs to her new attic quarters equipped with a pine low-poster bed with simple rounded mirror-top finals, a slender Victorian lift-top desk, a narrow six-drawer dresser with rounded knobs, a wash basin painted with the scene of a

Dutch windmill, and a white chamber pot. A brass warming pan leaned against the mantel of a small fireplace.

"One hour," instructed Agnes. "Down ... we meet about teach children." She left the room and Evalyn alone.

For the next few minutes, Erik struggled up the stairway with her remaining bag. The first time she met him on the top landing and offered help. "No," he stated firmly, glancing nervously down the stairwell. But then he offered her a slight smile and left the room. Evalyn understood. She began unpacking the schoolbooks, arranging them first in neat stacks from largest to smallest and according to subject. Then her sparse clothing was refolded and stacked into a few of the many dresser drawers. The bottom drawer, she decided, would be reserved for island treasures. She hoped to find a few interesting shells and other mysteries.

On the thin austere mantle sat a plain shelf clock with brass hands. Evalyn glanced at it every minute or so, careful to make certain to give herself a five-minute lead to descend the staircase and demonstrate punctuality. Already, she sensed Agnes to be an expedient, practical woman.

To begin the first day's teaching, Evalyn chose both an English and arithmetic primer. During the previous week, she had outlined a daily schedule and lesson plan: morning stretches while counting in English; English speaking, writing, and reading lessons, including penmanship and literature; arithmetic; a break for dinner; afternoon chores and possibly a walk on the island – during which science and geography would be introduced and discussed; and, finally, essays and question responses regarding world and American history. She hoped Agnes was amenable.

Evalyn smoothed her dress, pinched her cheeks, checked her hair in the tiny dresser mirror, and made her way to the parlor with books in hand. Agnes appeared from the hall, the children following. "May I address you as Mrs. Larsson?"

"Yes."

"May I show you a schedule?" Evalyn expected language barrier confusion, so she handed a neatly penned list toward Agnes, who stared at it blankly.

"If you need to take some time to …"

Abruptly, Agnes snatched the piece of paper, exited the home's front door, and headed toward the lighthouse. Evalyn tensed. The children appeared emotionless. They stood stiffly and patiently. Evalyn watched nonplussed out the window, gloom needling her mind. *Was it too much? Can she read? Does she think me obstinate for not asking her for a schedule? Is she going to give Mr. Larsson an earful?*

For Evalyn, the silent wait with the children was interminable. When the massive iron lighthouse door opened to reveal Agnes, followed by her husband, Evalyn's exhale was audible. She braced herself. Glancing at the children, she was surprised to see a gradual coloring of their faces. Their shoulders appeared to soften.

All that Evalyn could make out of Lias Larsson was his shadowy, sturdy figure as it followed Agnes up the wooden walkway. He held two large buckets and, though he wore thick flannel, the muscular bulk of his chest and arms was evident. She heard the buckets clank on the entryway stoop and she readied herself.

Agnes re-entered the home perturbed, but Lias immediately impressed relief upon the parlor scene. "So, I am to understand you are new teacher," he addressed Evalyn. She was immediately surprised by the quality of his English. He held out his hand, "Velcome. Velcome."

"Tha …nk you … sir," she said, righting her speech. "I am very pleased to be here, and I hope that I did not confuse or offend in any way. I was simply showing Mrs. Larsson an example of a teaching schedule that we might begin and continue through the week."

"Yes, of course. Let me view this. My wife simply vanted me to look. She is learning, still, the English."

Agnes directed a stern comment in Swedish to Lias. Unfazed, he continued reading the lesson plan. "Yes. Yes. This all seems vell and good. You start this teaching with the children and ve vill see the results, yes?"

Evalyn nodded, followed with, "Yes, Mr. Larsson, that is my sincere intention."

"The children, they learning English, too. They learn quickly. Only speak English to them. They only speak English back to you."

Evalyn nodded again, considering his statements; she knew no Swedish so the children would, indeed, have to speak English and learn to understand lessons in English.

Lias turned to Agnes and spoke gently to her in Swedish while at the same time placing a fatherly hand on her shoulder.

"Humph," she expressed, looking at both her children and Evalyn and then leaving the room through the passageway to the outdoor kitchen.

"My vife welcomes you, too. She has trouble with English and vishes Erik and Elsa to know to speak vell. She vishes that I tell you to teach them at dining table. She vishes to tell you to teach children about this island, Charleston, South Carolina, about America, and many English words. Children vill teach her vhat they know." He paused, smiling and ruffling the children's blond hair, "And teach me, too." He added exuberantly, "Ve love America and ve stay here."

Countenance relaxed, Evalyn offered Lias a slight smile.

He leaned down to meet his children's faces and began in Swedish, but then corrected himself, "... I ... er ... yes. Vhen you are finished some of the days, ve go in boat to get flounder. Yes?"

They beamed back at him. There was a tacit understanding between them.

In Lias' demeanor, Evalyn discerned surplus optimism and promise to compensate for what she already guessed was wanting in Agnes. She wondered how long into the marriage did he realize his role as sanguine partner.

When he righted himself, he turned toward Evalyn and announced, "I must vork and you must teach." Smiling, he saluted to the children as he left the home, only to disappear again behind the lighthouse door.

Evalyn eased the children into the first day's lessons, careful not to overwhelm. She allowed them to show her on slates the letters and words and numbers they already knew. She showed them a map of the islands, of South Carolina, and of the United States to give them a reference point. She had them repeat simple phrases. Hours flew by. Agnes appeared only to dismiss Evalyn from the dining room.

Exhausted by day's end, Evalyn allowed the children to lead her back to her attic room, where a slight supper of bread, cheese, and a few slices of pear awaited her on a small china plate. The children lingered, smiling at the doorway, and then Elsa said, "Happy ... night," before turning to leave. "Yes," added Erik. "Good ... night."

******

"Let us get started, shall we," Evalyn said to the children just after completing a simple breakfast the next morning. Agnes nodded toward Evalyn when she entered the dining room, but she did not speak. Lias, assumed Evalyn, was already in the lighthouse.

"This day we will have a full schedule. We will work there in the dining room and begin by studying English and writing and grammar," she announced to the children, unsure if they understood all her words. She removed primers out of her satchel. They seemed weighted with significance. Though she taught the day before, it had seemed a blur. The reality of where she was and what was before her straightened her spine and brightened her cheeks. *I'm a teacher*, she thought, a throaty giddiness yearning to break free.

For the rest of that morning on Morris Island, in the lighthouse family home, Evalyn spoke phrases, sentences, and short scriptures, and then she insisted her new charges repeat the words carefully and write them with chalk on their slates after they viewed what she had written on her own slate. Sometimes she gestured with her hands, pointed to an object, or drew simple sketches to help them ascertain meaning. She knew further understanding would come. She wanted them to ease into the comfort of the English words voiced and written.

Agnes floated in and out of the dining room. She watched Evalyn teach and sometimes sat and concentrated on the lesson for a few moments. Then she would rise and leave the room, disturbing Evalyn mid-instruction.

Elsa and Erik's enthusiasm for the lessons and evident acceptance of Evalyn motivated her to become more animated during

Agnes' absences from the room. Once during a short scripture reading, to demonstrate "fly on wings like eagles," Evalyn flapped her arms and turned in a close circle to "fly." However, she gasped, arms deflating to her side, when she realized Agnes peering through the window from outside. The mother's eyes were wide; brow furrowed. Evalyn turned to look at the children and immediately back to the window. Agnes had disappeared. Again, the children's faces appeared impervious. Evalyn, though, was muddled. She hurried into the next lesson phase, only to be interrupted by Elsa's rising hand.

"Toilette ... err commode?"

"Yes, of course. You too, Erik? You may be excused for a few moments."

As soon as the children left the room, Agnes appeared – as if lurking and waiting for the moment. Her pronouncement of "dinner" and a tray shoved in her direction, followed by "eat ... room ... teach 2 o'clock," made Evalyn realize the morning had flown by. She forced a flustered "thank you" to Agnes, who had already turned to leave the room.

In her quarters, Evalyn ate a slice of ham, mashed sweet potatoes, pickled okra, and a biscuit. She was hungry. Teaching, though not a physical endeavor, resulted in a voracious appetite. As she ate, she lingered on the morning and her awkwardness with Agnes. Evalyn considered that perhaps insecurity was the reason for her employer's odd behavior. Certainly, coming to a new country, experiencing an unfamiliar language, adapting to a different climate, residing on a lonely patch of land, allowing a stranger to teach her children … Anyone, even she, might behave unusually.

Evalyn sensed husband and children were solid clay to Agnes' sifting sand. Evalyn resolved she would try to be as well.

THE CHILDREN

Before Evalyn could blink, her first week of teaching on the island was in its last hour. She hoped the skiff arrived on time so she would not have to linger and endure Agnes' surveillance a moment longer than necessary. Although Evalyn felt her first week as teacher was an estimable success, the mother's irregularity drained her. One moment Agnes' facade was one of interest and approval, and then shortly thereafter – without warning – turned sour or bothered or even gloomy. Agnes sat, vigilant, in a corner knitting or embroidering; or, she busied herself around the home. But Evalyn often caught Agnes watching her. Sometimes her eyes would lower when Evalyn looked up, but other times the firm stare lasted a long second or two.

Evalyn sometimes passed the sitting room to view Agnes pouring over English lessons, whispering the pronunciation to herself. Evalyn instinctively dared not stop at the doorway. Occasionally, though, Evalyn detected a soft, affable expression spreading across Agnes' face. Yet it seemed to Evalyn that something worrisome always seemed to loiter on the perimeter.

Erik and Elsa were unruffled in their mother's presence. Evalyn, though roused inwardly, followed their cue. Unlike her negro pupils, whose innate response was to shrink from a steely glance or a harsh word, Evalyn's current charges conveyed a secure countenance. Either they had not experienced physical wrath from their mother, or their father's benevolence both overshadowed and balanced their mother's unpredictability.

Whatever the case, Evalyn admired Erik and Elsa. Already she was fond of them. And her first five days as their teacher flew by because of the sheer enjoyment of the work. She spent hours in her room each evening worrying over specific lessons; pondering meticulously over details. *Enough? Not enough? Conveyed correctly? Were they learning?* But when she stood or sat in front of them, Evalyn seemingly hovered outside herself as an observer of a supernatural spirit orchestrating each subject. Her students engaged, laughed, questioned, and beamed.

Neither favored their mother in personality or appearance. Erik shared his father's square jaw and thick cow-licked hair. The boy's shoulders and chest, too, were growing and broadening, bull-like. From her father, Elsa gleaned softer characteristics: smile lines at the corner creases of her eyes and at the bridge of her nose, and tresses glossy from sun exposure. Both children inherited his laugh, a joyous contagion to put at ease anyone in earshot. They devised harmless pranks and clever ditties just to prompt pleasurable amusement from their father during evening supper. In turn, he connived comebacks to prolong the mirth. The enjoyment the three built served to confirm a cohesive character trait to withstand the family's tempestuous maternal presence. Evalyn's inquisitive mind pondered endlessly these dynamics.

"You will return … Sunday?" Erik asked Evalyn Friday afternoon as he watched her pack; a tinge of apprehension infused his question.

On that Thursday, in front of Agnes and the children, Lias had asked Evalyn if she could settle into her room on Sunday early evening instead of Monday morning so that a full week's worth of teaching could take place and part of Monday would not be lost in traveling to the island. Evalyn thought Agnes bristled, and Lias had spoken a few words to his wife in Swedish. He had offered to add a small amount to Evalyn's wages to get her there on Sunday. Evalyn had declined. "It makes more sense for me to do that," she had agreed. "That will be fine."

"Yes, Sunday," Evalyn answered Erik. She straightened from packing in her valise a few weekend items. The children had followed her upstairs to "help." She smiled. *They will miss me.* "From 4 p.m. today until 5 p.m. Sunday, how many hours?"

"Forty-eight" shot Erik confidently. Elsa furrowed her brow, looked up thoughtfully, and blurted "49!"

"Correct, Elsa! Your arithmetic mind is sharp."

Erik frowned.

"But your language skills have improved even in one week," Evalyn encouraged the boy.

"Ve vill miss you," murmured Elsa, hands clasped, eyes downcast.

"Wa ... wa ... Elsa," scolded Erik, still smarting from the calculation error. "Say 'w'! We ... we will ... we will miss you."

Evalyn's look conveyed mild correction. Gently, she reiterated Erik's instruction.

"*We* will miss you," said Elsa. Her hands cupped her face and she released a sob. She left Evalyn's room and scurried down the stairs.

"Elsa, wait!" called Evalyn.

It was too late. Evalyn exited the room to witness Agnes accosting her daughter at the stair's base. Evalyn backed off the balcony and into her room. Erik dared not exit. They listened keenly. The barrage of words directed from mother to daughter was in Swedish. Erik, grasping lightly Evalyn's blouse sleeve, tapped his teacher on the shoulder and pulled on her sleeve. Evalyn leaned down and the boy's broken English translation, feather whispered in her ear, tickled the hairs on her neck:

What, child?

Nothing.

Do not say nothing. Who saddens?

No one, mama.

Go … get branch!

No, mama, please. I am sad. Teacher leaves.

Child! She is only worker … nothing … nothing more!

Erik released his hand from Evalyn's sleeve and took a step back. With his hands behind his back and his head slightly bowed, he said, "We will see you … Sunday. Forty *nine* hours."

******

"Have you completed your foolish experiment?" asked Evalyn's mother. It was dark inside the home but for the candle on the side table next to the rocking chair where her mother sat mending a sock.

"The week was fruitful, thank you."

"So, you plan to return?"

"Yes, mother. I am a teacher now."

"You have work here, too. I will leave it in your basket for you to do tomorrow."

"I must prepare lesson plans, mother. I am no longer a seamstress."

"You will return to your proper work at each week's end if you are to stay here. Your fath … We agreed."

For a few stunned seconds, Evalyn stared at the woman in the corner. Her mother stayed fixed on the needle and sock. The stepfather's snore emanated from behind the wall. It was his practice to sleep when it was dark and awake when it was light. He did not read or converse by candlelight.

"Is there a bit of supper still?" asked Evalyn.

"You know that we sup early, especially in winter."

Evalyn took that as a no.

With bag still in hand, she turned toward the spare bedroom. "Good night, mother." Evalyn received no reply.

******

"Mizerab fanm," was a favorite expression of Samuel's. It was what entered Evalyn's mind as soon as she awoke that first Saturday morning upon returning to James Island.

When she walked to Mac's later that morning, she was surprised to overhear, while purchasing thread for her mother and a few sheets of paper for the children, that the miners were given a few days furlough from the phosphate mines in Charleston due to winter's low demand for fertilizer. At home, she sped through the pile of assigned mending, leaving the sewing of a shift and a bed gown for the pastor's wife until mid-afternoon. The mild, sunny, January day invited a walk. At McLeod's, Evalyn found Samuel wrestling some of the younger boys in the dirt lot outside one of the small former-slave cabins.

"Evalyn!" cried Samuel, prying a five-year-old off one of his legs. "Scoots you's!"

"They are glad to have their Samuel home," said Evalyn, suppressing a temptation to throw her arms around him.

"I'm the only one fool hardy 'nough to play wif 'em," he laughed. "Work, work, work's all its been 'bout on this here place. Least theys gettin' paid now."

"Samuel! Mind your speech!"

"Oh, I apologize, your teacher highness. My speech doth descend when I am in the presence of only laborers and not the learned."

"Samuel, you have not given up on your dream to teach as well, I hope."

"Not given up, no! But I must continue on in the mines for a bit longer to save the money I need for the northern college. Did I tell you I wrote to Wilberforce and they will take me? I will do it, God willing."

"You will make a fine teacher and give so many hope for a future of their own. But what is it like in the mines? Is it terrible, Samuel?"

His shirt sleeves were rolled to the elbows and her eyes lingered guiltily on his forearms' defined muscles.

"They just took the same way of working slaves in the fields to the mines. They give me a task; I finish it. That task gets noted. The only difference – I get paid for those completed tasks. A ditch gets me about 30 cents on the dollar per foot. Shoveling and hauling that rock, a little more … not much. I lead the men in hymn singin'. Think about college … think about standin' up in front of a classroom teachin'."

"But the dangers?"

"Not too much. Freedmen used to the hot, but Scals cannot abide. The cool north is in their blood. And if someone's droppin' from the fever, it's a Scal mostly. Haitian blood is my armor. Those mosquitoes are not giving me the sickness! And the phosphate stuck on creek's bottom, with the oyster shells and such, local boys know how to dive in there and work them out. Scals scared of what's in the muck. They have to stay in the boat and sort through the marl and such so baskets just get filled with the good rocks. I don't know if it's better than field work. Pays more though."

"My plight is quite different. My first week teaching at the lighthouse was more than agreeable. But I have two harsh women with which to contend." Evalyn sat down on a rough-hewn bench and told

Samuel, who perched on a nearby log, of her mother's objections and her employer's volatility.

"Yes, they are *mizerab fanm*. You remember the Creole? Sad women. Miserable. Their misery spills over onto the lives of others. You are anizan fanm … a pleasant woman. Do not get caught in their *mizerb* web." He winked at her, and the simple eye movement rushed blood to her cheeks.

"Oh, but the children, Samuel," she managed, willing her hands not to cradle her flushed face. "They are precious already to me …. so precious. They are like their father, who is a lively man. Their hair is the color of the whitest shells and their Swedish voices so lyrical. Oh, Samuel, it is all that I imagined teaching would be – and I've only just begun, truly."

No one on the plantation minded the two. Evalyn noted the bustle about the old place: varying degrees of clanking coming from the barn; hammering just outside the home; the swoosh of brooms on wooden floors. A few children climbed, and swung, and giggled on branches of the giant sentry oaks lining the drive. Some of the older, formerly enslaved had known her father. They acknowledged Evalyn with a "Hi, Miss Eva" or a simple nod. Young ones had been her test pupils; these children skittered shyly to the corners of cottages and observed. Some waved, giggled, and disappeared. She felt a slight shameful stab at abandoning their teaching.

Her unease became audible. "Will you encourage these children to practice reading while you are here? They need to see how important it is to you. Is there anyone living here who can do some regular lessons?"

"Yes, I will. And I will think on the right person. Now that you are a *real* teacher!" He picked up a branch and poked playfully at her side.

People in the yard looked on, but none thought beyond Samuel and "Miss Eva" as friends – it just was; always had been.

"Oh, Samuel, I am sorry that I am no longer able to teach the children here. But it is so rewarding to be paid … to truly be a professional teacher. To have a salary for doing what you love. I want that for you."

Samuel smiled. He stared at Evalyn for a moment without speaking. She felt another rush to her cheeks.

When a woman walked into a side yard and pulled up collards, Evalyn noted the hour. Cleaning, stripping stems, chopping, boiling, and setting to simmer a pot of collards with a bit of fatback for flavor took time before the supper call. Evalyn glanced at the sun's placement for confirmation. She needed to return home to finish sewing by daylight instead of candlelight.

She rose to leave. "I'm praying God will multiply your money like he did the loaves and the fishes."

"Lordy, that would be some miracle now!" he laughed. "Would like to see that! You take care now. Stay out of lighthouse lady's way!"

Samuel stood to watch her leave. Before she reached McLeod's carriage entrance, Samuel sprinted gazelle-like to her side. Evalyn startled. "Seriously though, stay out of the way of *mizerab fanm*. Withhold your joy when she is around. Be a teacher only, while she watches. That is your job."

Evalyn, wide-eyed, opened her mouth to speak. But Samuel's long legs were already carrying him back toward the cottages. Children ran to him and he scooped up two. He waved an arm to her but did not turn around.

******

The sun's light fractured the morning. Into Evalyn's room it streamed severely, overwhelming any shadows. *Solis gravibus.*

It was another temperate January day. She was back on Morris Island. She searched her room for the small instructional Latin book she kept on the nightstand. She pulled the lace curtains across the window to filter the stark light so that the room's items became clearer. The light exposed the dark leather-covered book on the floor beside her bed. Evalyn straightened and smoothed her skirt and apron and tucked behind pins the stray hairs about her face.

Arrival the previous evening, with no presence or greeting from Agnes, flustered Evalyn. Erik met her at the dock to take her small bag. He smiled wide in her direction when his back was to the house. But when he turned toward the home on the weathered wooden walkway, his mood sobered. There was no sign of Elsa. Lias, she assumed, was in the lighthouse. Erik took her bag directly to her room – already glowing from the oil lamp, even though a little of dusk's light still penetrated. Without a word, he pulled the door closed behind him. A small plate of bread, a few stewed oysters, and one-half of a preserved peach awaited her as supper.

Evalyn slept fitfully. Her dreams anticipated pessimistically the new week. Yet, when she woke, she lit the oil lamp, managed her toilette, and reached for her bible. Though reading through Romans daily, so that she could pass on the book's rich truths to the children, she decided to meditate on whatever passage was revealed in the opening. A favorite in Ephesians, and a comfort after the long night:

"… when anything is exposed by the light, it becomes visible, for anything that becomes visible is light. 'Awake, O sleeper, and arise from the dead, and Christ will shine on you.' Look carefully then how you walk, not as unwise, but as wise."

Evalyn read the passage over, carefully pondering its implication afresh. *He means to assure me*, she thought, interpreting the scriptures. *I need not be rattled. Only teach, as I was hired to teach. Teach, as Samuel reminded. What is to be lain bare will be lain bare.*

She ascertained "walk" as confirmation of an idea manifested on the boat ride to the island. On pleasant days, she would insist at least some part of the school day taking place while walking along the shore and wooded paths. Breathing in fresh air and incorporating into lessons the natural surroundings would help the children learn.

Evalyn righted herself, gathered supplies, and walked self-assuredly down the pine steps. She entered the dining room cautiously. The children were seated, as was Lias, who the previous week was already in the lighthouse during breakfast. Agnes' back was to Evalyn and she leaned toward her husband as he whispered in Swedish, his hand clutching gently his wife's arm. A floorboard groaned under Evalyn's step and Agnes turned.

"Sit. Sit," she instructed, pulling a chair out for Evalyn. A forced smile strained the edges of Agnes' mouth. "Ve are happy teacher is back. Yes, children? Yes?"

"Yes, Mor, yes," said the children in unison.

"Mama. In America, mama, yes?"

"Yes, Mama," they answered, smiling up at her.

Lias, too, beamed – his expression genuine.

Evalyn discerned his presence. It was clear to her that he was present at the breakfast table to temper his wife.

The meal Agnes set before them communicated a purposeful and cheery countenance as well: hot cakes, fresh bread, sausages, and fried potatoes. A contrast to the cold corn bread and soft-boiled eggs she was given to eat in her room alone the week prior.

Initially, the only sounds in the modest dining room were of chewing and swallowing, the tink of cutlery, and wood crackling in the fireplace. Evalyn eyed Lias, who prompted his wife with the nod of his head. Agnes turned suddenly to Evalyn. "You are rested from Sat-tur-

day and Sun-day, yes?" The corners of her mouth turned slightly —
another attempt at a smile.

"Yes. Thank you."

Satisfied, Agnes spoke to her husband in Swedish, and with
another attempt toward hospitality asked Evalyn, "You need ... for
your room, anything?"

"No. I have everything I need. Thank you."

There was more conversation in Swedish between husband and
wife as the children ate their breakfast quietly; all food on their plates
disappeared gradually.

"We are so thankful you are here," Lias said, suddenly. He laid
his hand lightly over his wife's while he spoke. "We want that our
children be e-quip ... e-quipped. Is that correct word?"

"Yes."

"... equipped for lives in America," he continued. "You are
teacher who will do that. Thank you. If anything you need Miss Gray,
... anything, please alert me or my wife." He patted gently Agnes' hand
while making eye contact with her. He spoke to her in Swedish.
Translation, assumed Evalyn.

"I would like to ask if I can take the children outside to do lessons on days when temperatures are agreeable."

The word "outside" piqued Erik and Elsa's attention; they both looked up in unison from their plates. Their faces anticipated a response.

Evalyn noticed instantly Agnes' expression sour. But Lias' hand, still atop his wife's, squeezed tenderly before he spoke: "Yes. That is good idea. They get fresh air and know island. You teach them history of this place and all animals and birds and trees and plants. Yes? They learn these in English."

"Exactly," said Evalyn, a bit too boisterously. She toned down enthusiasm to continue, "And they will learn some Latin names and words, also. Latin is the basis for many words in science and English, and their minds will be strong. Is that agreeable?"

"Yes. Yes."

Agnes removed her hand from beneath her husband's, yet she turned toward Evalyn and offered a taut smile as a tacit response. She moved the bowl with remaining potatoes in Evalyn's direction and asked, "Eat more, yes?"

"No, thank you." Then to the children, Evalyn said, "We will begin arithmetic inside the home this morning and later will move remaining studies out of doors as long as the weather holds."

Evalyn's second week of teaching on Morris Island was to be the warmest in memory, according to James Islanders' predictions, which she overheard during the previous weekend's furlough. The break from typical bleak winter weather afforded her full advantage of an outdoor classroom. While in eyeshot of the house, Evalyn led Erik and Elsa in a line, careful to gesture and point and ask them to write responses on their slates. But when trees obscured them from tepid observation, Evalyn modeled an infectious liveliness, stomping through fluffs of gray meringue-like foam at low tide, digging with sticks at fiddler crab burrows in an attempt to expose the tiny crustaceans, or emulating with her arms various birds' wing movements. When packed flocks of black birds rose and fell like a hung sheet billowing in the wind, Evalyn would rise on her toes, sway from right to left, and lift her open palms to conduct the skyward orchestra.

She encouraged deep inhalations and described the origin of various briny scents.

Initially, when Evalyn taught with physical expression, Erik and Elsa eyed her warily. The pupils soon relaxed into her playful teaching style. They studied every proper name of visible plants, birds, animals, and fish. Shoreline flounder, eyes staring eerily from one side, became disturbed from shallow sandy hiding places when the children were taught to poke them with long sticks. Elsa squealed when one moved; Erik laughed loud like his father. Evalyn required them to write proper names on their slates and speak them back several times. The first time she spelled the name for them, and then it became a game for the siblings to see who could rewrite the name the fastest and spell it correctly.

They scrutinized for long moments marsh shell beds and beaches, verbalizing every detail of sight and sound. Later, Evalyn would help them write sense-of-place paragraph essays, enabling them to communicate details through quill and ink onto paper. These short narrations, she decided, would be read in practiced English during the supper hour.

She taught them to distinguish marsh and beach areas riddled with razor-sharp oyster shells, which could damage shoes' leather soles and slice bare feet. The oyster beds and shelves she dubbed treacherous zones to be avoided as a rule.

Evalyn noticed Erik's protection over his sister. He boasted when he bested her at answers, but then grabbed her hand to guide her onto a path. During short breaks, Erik offered Elsa sips from his water flask. Evalyn let them stray, a little. She watched the pair picking up shells, sharing excitedly each discovery. She sat on bleached driftwood and enjoyed them jesting while drawing pictures and writing messages in the sand with long sticks. She made them learn, but she also let them play.

They enjoyed especially discussing hunting habits of egrets, resplendent and plentiful on Morris Island. From densely packed nests, the great snowy birds scattered to seemingly assigned designations throughout marshes and along shores, only to return en masse before dusk. Internal clocks motivated the stick-legged hunters – no matter the weather or the season. The ecosystem was science, Evalyn explained, but it was God's first. The balance of the tides and patterns of live activity was His breathing in and out over the water and the land.

Evalyn knew the fraying language barrier allowed the children to comprehend only bits and pieces, but it would all make sense eventually.

"Why gray water when gray sky," asked Erik, when unwelcome austereness violated their formerly sunny day.

"The water reflects the sky," taught Evalyn. "Gray above, gray below – gray on the horizon." She pointed to vastness.

"I like blue water, blue sky," said Elsa.

"But there is beauty, even in the gray," assured their teacher.

In time, the children knew when they returned home from these excursions to "straighten up," as Evalyn initially told them, before detection by their mother, who always seemed vexed at their arrival. Agnes watched for the returning party from a window and waited with towel in hand to rough-wipe sand accumulated on their shoes and around the hem of Erik's pants and Elsa's skirt. In the presence of their mother, they restrained any zeal experienced during outdoor lessons.

"Attend to chores," was her welcome. The children complied gravely. They anticipated their father's cheerful green light during evening meals. Approval of educational jaunts was apparent in Lias' jovial expression and boisterous demand to "show me with your words what you learn today!" He laughed generously and encouraged lengthy supper table discourse.

Contained gall emanated from Agnes as the children shared and her husband encouraged. She feigned endorsement with slight nods and even slighter smiles.

Evalyn ended her second week in the Larssons' employ satisfied with her young, eager learners but greatly perplexed by the mystery of their mother's nettled spirit.

THE KEEPER

Creek water, still as reflective glass when flanked by marsh grass, grew anxious and rippling as it merged with its salty ocean neighbor. Evalyn approached her third week with the Larssons surer of herself and her role on the island. Sand bars far off on the horizon broke waves that dissipated before they came anywhere near the lighthouse.

Evalyn noticed another small boat anchored at the dock. She detected Erik as well. He waved to her, a smile broad on his pale face. She looked beyond the dock for Agnes.

"We have visitors," called Erik, even before the boat reached him.

"I see."

"Lighthouse men ... come to meet Papa," adding, "Mama feeds them now." He extended his hand.

"Ah," said Evalyn, reaching for his hand. "You are quite the young gentleman."

Erik's cheeks flushed pink. He picked up her bag from the dock – her taxi boat already turned for its return trip. He took the lead to the house. "Ve … we, sorry, have surprise for you."

"Oh? And you must add the article 'a' before surprise. A surprise."

"Sorry."

"Remember. No need for apologies. Only correct next time and I know you are learning."

"Yes, Miss Gray." He glanced back at her. "You will like a surprise, yes? Your lessons help us to make."

"I love surprises! *Good* surprises."

"This is good one."

"A good one."

"Yes," laughed Erik. "A good surprise."

Just inside the doorway to the right, the dining room hosted Lias and two other men. Agnes was setting steaming bowls and platters on the table. Evalyn started for the stairway, following Erik, who was already halfway up with her bag.

"Miss Gray," called Lias. "You must meet."

Evalyn turned, smoothed her skirt and secured hair pins.

She entered the dining room to greet three standing men she supposed were all around the same age.

"Miss Gray, teacher to children, this is Angus Bennett and Thomas O'Hagan. Mr. Bennett, he was lighthouse keeper here. He keeps lighthouse at Georgetown now. Mr. O'Hagan is just there," he pointed northward toward the window, "across the channel … Sullivan's Island lighthouse."

Agnes hovered at Evalyn's side, a basket of biscuits in her hand. "You supper in room," she whispered, firmly.

"Yes, ma'am. So nice to meet you gentleman. I hope your stay here will be fruitful. Good evening."

As Evalyn ascended the stairs, she heard the men settling back into their dining chairs and an attempted whisper from one of the men: "She seems a lovely girl."

"Lovely, yes," responded Lias.

Evalyn cringed. She hoped Agnes had returned to the kitchen.

"You are fortunate to have a young woman willing to come here and teach the children weekly," said O'Hagan. "Because this lighthouse stands on an island, it has been difficult to keep help. Most lighthouses edge mainlands. No need to take a boat to get to them."

"Yes. We are blessed. Yes, dear?" prompted Lias.

"Yes. Ve … we are blessed," Agnes responded, unyieldingly.

"You must sit," insisted Lias. "All food is here. We bless and we eat."

Agnes leaned in to speak to him in Swedish.

Resigned, Lias announced, "She will sup in kitchen area. She wants for us to speak of lighthouse matters."

Evalyn slipped into her room behind Erik. Elsa stood just inside the door, a small parcel in her outstretched hand. She radiated a welcome.

"What's this?" Evalyn sat down on her bed and pulled the twine bow. Wrapped inside crinkled brown paper, undoubtedly left over from an old Christmas gift, was a small hand-made book. Evalyn studied the cover, *Lessons and Life* by Erik and Elsa Larsson. The hand-drawn cover illustration was of the lighthouse, waves in the background and a sunset far off on the horizon. Turning each page gingerly, she welled with pride at the tangible evidence of their learning. One or the other's drawings and narration filled the pages; complete sentences, though simple, shared with the reader information about the snowy egret, fiddler crabs, sea oats, lettered olive shells, flounder, and more.

"I absolutely love it," said Evalyn. In her enthusiasm, she opened her arms for an embrace. When she realized their uncertainty, she dropped her arms. But Elsa stepped shyly toward her. "I am so proud of you," said Evalyn, drawing her in. "That is the best surprise ever," she directed to Erik. She reached out her hand and ruffled his hair. "You two get the 'best pupils' award! Thank you!"

"Papa gave us paper," offered Elsa.

"Yes. We tell him of plans and he is happy about this," said Erik.

Evalyn resisted the temptation to correct grammar. "So, this week I would like to be a pupil as well." She laughed lightly at their confused expressions.

"I do not understand," said Elsa, still leaning warmly into her.

Evalyn stood up from the bed. "Did you know that the best way to learn is to teach. So, teach me all you know about the lighthouse. And what you do not know, we will learn together. Agreed?"

Bright faces beamed approval.

The next day, a storm threatened. Bennett and O'Hagan, who planned an early morning inspection and a recitation of updates to *Instructions to Employees of the United States Lighthouse Service*, before returning to their own postings, decided to stay and assist Lias. Unspoken was their intention to view his methods. Lighthouse keeping was in the visitors' fibers; both were fathered by keepers. They knew little about the Swede, other than what was in writing and what they saw of his character. There was no one to assist Lias, after More Wilkinson slipped and shattered his ankle just after the Larsson family's arrival to Morris Island. Isolation deterred so many from consideration of the lighthouse life. Bennett and O'Hagan both had assistants – backup, accountability, reprieve. So far, however, they were unable to find someone to shadow Lias. The two men agreed: their report to the Lighthouse Board (ultimately passed onto Congress) would include their first-hand observation of Lias under pressure, and his skills at guiding safely approaching vessels bound for Charleston Harbor. They would spend another night and leave the island in the morning, weather permitting.

Most days, Lias wore a basic cotton dungaree blouse and trousers; sometimes, when a laborious repair task was required, he donned overalls. With colleagues present, Lias' dress for the day was the same as his guests': navy blue dress jacket, double-breasted flannel sack coat with a double row of gilt buttons, matching navy blue trousers and vest, black tie with pressed white shirt, black shined leather shoes, and a conical, flat-top navy blue cap. As they exited the home in the dawn's early light, they appeared, to Evalyn, to be Naval men of distinction. However, USLHS, embroidered on their jackets, distinguished them not as military men but as men of the United States Lighthouse Service.

They moved with authority toward the entryway of the lighthouse and disappeared within the tower's gaping mouth. Evalyn knew the light was extinguished early each morning. One need only to look up. No movement; no light. What else Lias did all day was a mystery to her. She intended to ask – as part of their lessons.

The opportunity came at mid-day when the party entered the home, closing behind them cold wind and a darkening sky. Arithmetic, Latin, and English books were cleared from the dining table, and Elsa was employed to help Agnes with the meal. Erik was charged with bringing in more firewood. Guests dictated formality for the normally unceremonious milieu.

Evalyn retreated to her room. She startled when Lias' voice bellowed up the stairwell: "Please, Miss Gray, join us this day."

"Sir," she said, peeking out her door into the stairwell.

"Yes, please. We wish to speak to you."

She hesitated.

"Miss? Yes … please join dinner this day."

"Yes, sir."

Satisfied, Lias left the stairwell. Evalyn smoothed her skirt and adjusted her hair, glancing quickly in the dresser mirror at her nonplussed expression. What would Agnes think of the invitation?

Evalyn walked slowly down the stairs and entered solemnly the dining room. Agnes was setting a bowl of peach preserves and biscuits on the table. Her husband stood and pulled the chair out beside him. "Sit," he instructed Agnes, giving her no time to protest. O'Hagan pulled out the chair beside him, smiling widely at Evalyn. Agnes did not acknowledge the teacher.

"Mr. Bennett, would honor with blessing?" asked Lias.

"Certainly."

Bless O Lord, this food to our use,

And us to thy loving service;

And make us ever mindful of the needs of others,

For Jesus' sake. Amen.

"Thank you, sir. And Miss Gray ..." addressed Lias as he raised his head from the reverential bow, "my guests ask if you and if children know about lighthouse ..."

"It is our desire," interrupted Bennett, "that all children of lighthouse keepers learn much of the inner workings of the lighthouse, the role of the lighthouse keeper, and the importance of the work. Proper writing and advancement in arithmetic is all well and good, Miss Gray, but these children are unlike other children. They are unlike other pupils. It behooves them to undergo the education of their father's chosen profession. Do you agree?"

"Yes, indeed. Yes, ... in fact ..."

"It is often the case that sons will follow as keepers and daughters as keepers' wives," added O'Hagan. "So, we think of it as a life lesson."

"Indeed," managed Evalyn. "This is coincidental, as I was just informing the children last evening that I would like for a portion of our lessons to include lighthouse education."

"Excellent!" shared the keeper guests.

"You are smart teacher," said Lias. "We will have smart children dear. Yes?" He turned toward Agnes, who stood abruptly, disturbing the china and glassware on the clothed table and scraping her chair loudly as she pushed it back.

"Vinegar!" she said, too loudly, a nervous scowl on her face. "I forget for greens." She exited the dining room.

Evalyn noticed the keeper guests glance at one another and then at Lias to understand his reaction. He and the children shared none. Their attention was on their plates as they ate.

"So, Miss Gray, we will tell you … But you have questions first, perhaps?" asked Lias, looking up from his plate seconds after his wife's exit.

"I don't even understand how it is lit, or how the light spins," she answered, her enthusiasm apparent.

Agnes returned and set down loudly the vinegar carafe. She was ignored by the others as she settled uneasily back into her chair and appeared to pay no attention to the discourse. Instead, she stooped exaggeratedly over her plate.

"Allow me," said O'Hagan. "I am newest to keeping, so this is fresh from *the* book. There is a giant wick, which gets trimmed and then lighted. The lighthouse light is truly a massive oil lamp. Do you understand what I am saying," he turned his attention toward the wide-eyed children, who nodded their heads.

"I have told them of some of this, but we have been here such short time that I have not taken time to instruct properly," interjected Lias, apologetically.

"There is no concern," continued O'Hagan. "There are large weights, see," he demonstrated with his hands, "and these weights are dropped down the tower shaft. Above, near the Fresnel … I mean the lens, there are the driving gears. When your father unlocks these weights at dusk and hand cranks them up to the top …" O'Hagan gestured dramatically as if pulling and straining. "… a new descent of the weight starts and turns the gear."

The children expressed no emotion.

"Do you understand children?" asked Evalyn. "Perhaps he speaks too quickly for you?"

"I understand … some … I think," answered Erik. He spoke in Swedish to his father.

Elsa nodded while her brother spoke. Then Erik summarized his understanding in simple English statements.

"Yes!" assured Lias. "You are correct."

"Well done," approved Bennett. "Remind me to task you, son, with new recruit instructions."

The men laughed.

"Your Papa is very strong," said O'Hagan. "We lighthouse keepers must be strong!" He pointed to his bicep.

The children giggled.

Agnes remained stoic, concentrating on deliberation of her meal.

"At dawn, we off the lamp by turning off the fuel that had kept the wick burning throughout the night," said O'Hagan, speaking more slowly for the children's benefit. "Just as if you are extinguishing the oil lamp at your beside. The weights are stopped and locked. And the Fresnel stops turning."

"Why do you name lens Fres … nel?" asked Elsa, timidly.

"Good question," answered Lias. "A Frenchman named Fresnel invented lens. Sorry, but too many words must explain this." He rose and left the room, returning with a small booklet. "I will translate this part to them in Swedish, and Miss Gray, you may take this to your room to read later."

"Gentleman, your meal … cold, with talk," inserted Agnes, whose plate was cleaned of food.

"Yes, dear. I will tell the children this quickly, and then we will eat and speak after."

What Lias read to the children in Swedish, and Evalyn devoured later in her room, fascinated her inquisitive mind: *The Fresnel lens consists of concentric rings of glass prisms that bend the light coming from a lamp inside the lens into a narrow beam. This lens has 1,176 prisms and 24 bullseyes. At the center, the bullseyes work like a magnifying glass so that the light beam is even more powerful. The lens sections are held together by brass frames weighing five to six tons. The entire lens weighs in at approximately six to eight tons.*

Bread pudding and coffee consumed, appreciation for the meal expressed, the men excused themselves from the table. "Swells are building," said Lias, looking out the window while pulling on his wool sack coat. A weathervane atop an outbuilding spun and changed direction. As he opened the door, it tugged against his weight with a full blast of wind.

To Evalyn, climbing the stairs to her room, Lias said, "You ask good questions. Teach children some terms from book. Maybe they learn to spell them and I test children on meaning." He winked at Evalyn.

"Send the children to the base with sandwiches and cider at nightfall, Agnes. Please. Thank you." He pulled the door closed and the men drew their coats around them as they maneuvered the boardwalk to the lighthouse.

Evalyn had only a few moments to toilette and return downstairs to resume afternoon lessons, but she pulled her bible off the bedside table and sat down in a rocking chair positioned by the room's window. With only gray light, she found familiar verses – though she knew them by heart –to decimate the unwanted, yet desirous pinch that occurred spontaneously the instant Lias winked at her. She ascertained his action reflected only a buoyant nature, which is why the momentary flutter disturbed her. *Search me and know me* ... she whispered, head bowed.

The storm, all gruff and no real substance, still served to satisfy the visitors' suppositions regarding their foreign colleague's skills and work ethic. Bennett and O'Hagan left the next morning confident that the Morris Island lighthouse was in capable hands. They promised to assign him an assistant as soon as a "quality man" was found, and they reminded Lias to signal immediately if an emergency proved too much for him to handle alone.

After the visitors left, Lias disappeared inside the lighthouse and made appearances only for meals and rest.

It was not until Friday morning, another clement winter day — still and bright — that Lias entered the home mid-morning, suspending memorization of the Declaration of Independence's natural laws introduction. Evalyn had chosen it and the Constitution's preamble as a combined history and English lesson. Erik exhaled loudly his approval of the interruption.

"Come. Come," said Lias. "I have completed much work this week and this morning is free for me to show you Fresnel."

Agnes bounded into the room, an article of clothing and thread and needle still in her hand. She started speaking in Swedish, paused, and then said in English, "Lias, no. Children have studies. Miss Gray leaves later."

"You come, too," he said, approaching her and grabbing her arm. "Today, this is part of the lighthouse school, yes?"

"No! I have mending." Visibly irked, she returned to the small drawing room.

"I will take you again later," he called after her. "I will show teacher and children now and Mama later, yes?" He smiled at the threesome, impervious to his wife's chafed will.

The door closed behind them and Evalyn caboosed the procession across the wooden walkway that hovered just inches above the sandy ground and toward the impressive brick stairway to the eight-foot steel door. Evalyn glanced just slightly toward the home. She detected movement at the window. Erik ascended the steps behind his father and waited for him to unlock the large brass padlock stamped with the naval insignia of an eagle, wings spread, with a faint outline of a ship at its back.

"I always lock," Lias explained as he inserted the key. "Even if gone only one minute. No chances ..." He explained, "No one must come in, ever, without me. Understand?" He did not wait for compliance but proceeded up a few more stairs.

Erik reached for his sister's hand, took her alongside their father, and transferred its daintiness into Lias' waiting palm. Next, he offered assistance to Evalyn. The quartet stepped carefully over a foot-tall metal threshold.

"You must be safe," instructed Lias. "You must do what I do."

He stood at the base, looking up, as if seeing the lighthouse core for the first time. Perforated metal steps wound like a reverse Dante's inferno, upward and out of site. Shafts of sunlight penetrating the few narrow windows enhanced the dramatic effect. The spiraling reminded Evalyn of the prettiest shell she had ever found, the nautilus. *Fitting*, she thought, wondering if the symbolic design was intentional to the Greek's origins. Lias allowed his small tour group to take in the site.

"We climb, yes?" asked Elsa, her voice emitting a faint shudder.

"Yes, we climb," answered Lias, extending a hand. "Stay close to wall and hold railing. Do not look down. One step, next step, until top. Erik, get behind Elsa. Help her and Miss Gray."

"I need no help," said Elsa, a quiver belying her expressed confidence. But when Lias moved toward the first main step, his hand grasping hers, she failed to move.

"I am looking more." Strain lines formed around the edges of her mouth. *Her mother's*, observed Evalyn.

"We will count the steps together," whispered Lias, leaning down and kissing his daughter on the cheek. "Your Papa, he makes this journey many times, yes? I will make you safe."

Like a funeral procession, the four began their gradient climb. Erik's darting eyes and open mouth disclosed awe. Elsa's stared only at her father's back.

"Feel the bricks, children. Each one made by hand. Dirt baked hard. How many?"

"500," answered Elsa, her voice muffled by her father's shirt.

"Thousands and thousands!" corrected Erik.

Lias did not answer but glanced and smiled at Evalyn. She returned a smile. Though she could feel her knees trembling a little more with each step, she thrilled at the adventure. Outside was a known world; inside the mighty brick and steel edifice was risk and mystery. Both exertion and zeal brightened her face. She suppressed the urge to giggle.

"You know echo, yes?" Lias asked, stopping at one of the two windows.

"Truly, I was just wondering whether an echo was possible," answered Evalyn.

"Yes, you try."

An impish grin grew across her face. "Yes?" she directed toward her wide-eyed pupils.

"Yes!" they shouted in unison, their voices reverberating briefly.

"HELLO!" shouted Evalyn, clearly and with all the thrust she could muster. The word bounced upward, repeating over and over until fading like a windswept ghost.

"Me!" said Erik; and, without waiting for a green light screamed "ERIK!"

"You try, darling," instructed Lias.

Elsa released her hold on her father's shirt, cupped her hands, and bellowed, "LIGHTHOUSE!"

The children sniggered at their folly. Lias began to laugh heartily, which stimulated unrestrained peals of laughter from Evalyn. The children followed suit, and for several seconds the group enjoyed their unhindered moment.

"Can our voices be heard from below," asked Evalyn, suddenly aware of herself.

"No," answered Lias. "We are safe here." He winked at her.

The transient gesture communicated volumes.

"Look how far we have come," said Lias, encouraging the party to look out the three-paned arched window before continuing.

Evalyn looked for Agnes. She saw no movement in or around the home below.

For the next several steps, no one spoke. The only sound was shoe leather on metal.

Evalyn boasted internally that the increasing height did not affect her. She was proud as well of the children's resolve, even little Elsa's.

"The light is extinguished," boomed Lias suddenly. Feeling the jerk of his daughter's being, he offered, "Forgive me. I forget. So loud. I am not often speaking as I climb." He continued in a more subdued tone to share knowledge. "But a keeper's tasks are more than light on, light off. I must clean and polish large lens every day. Wait until you view this! So large! And I must cover lens to protect it from sun. That is irony. Children, do you understand word … irony? Miss Gray, I learn this word is same in Swedish. We spell i-r-o-n-i. Do you know, children?"

"Yes," they answered in unison. "Miss Gray makes us know this," added Erik. "Irony. Fish breath in water, die on land. People live on land, die in water. But water meets land."

"Yes!" exclaimed Lias. "So smart. Children … I am proud Papa! Miss Gray is such fine teacher! Well, there is irony with Fresnel lens. It must burn bright, so bright at night. But it remains dark and covered during day. The bright sun may discolor prisms of lens. I must protect with lens bag from light of day so it burns bright at night. Irony! Yes?"

"Yes, Papa," they answered again together.

Lias' strong hand held fast to his daughter's as they climbed.

"What else is your work, Papa," she asked, earlier alarm dissipating.

"I must bring oil. Your Papa has strong arms from carrying. I must write … write all that I see of clouds and wind and waves. I must write reports. I must make repairs."

He stopped at a platform that bridged from one inner wall to another. "Do not look down, children. Look ahead or up. We are here."

They lined up along the bridge. Despite the warning, Evalyn braved a look below. Instantly, she swayed. Lias' arm shot out and he grasped firmly her forearm.

"Oh!"

"Please, Miss Gray. Do not look down."

"Yes, sorry."

His eyes searched hers. "You are fine, yes?"

Flushed by a twinge of nausea, and from embarrassment, she hesitated before answering him.

"Yes. Thank you. We can continue."

Above the bridge was a ship's ladder with railings on either side.

"A few more steps and you will be in lantern room," Lias announced eagerly. "And then you will see it ... the light. You first, darling. Careful now. Stand in room and wait for me. Miss Gray ..." He held out his hand. She took it and allowed him to deposit her onto the first rung of the ladder.

"Erik. Yes, son. Very good. Come, Elsa." Lias followed closely behind his children and Evalyn, and they all passed into the room darkened by the lens curtain. Lias pulled the linen lens cover off, folded it neatly, and placed it inside a nearby open crate.

The children and their teacher drew in audible breaths. "It is a big eye!" said Elsa.

"It is so big," added Erik. Evalyn made a mental note to teach her students synonyms for the word "big." That they were expressing any adjectives in their second language was an accomplishment, she reminded herself.

When the Fresnel lens was revealed, descriptive words inundated her learned mind: *magnificent, glorious, startling, engrossing, rapturous*. It struck Evalyn that it also resembled a giant's eye – the hollowed monolith, a Cyclops. Yet, instead of fearsome, Evalyn thought it spectacularly beautiful.

"You like, yes?" asked Lias, expectantly.

Her awe radiated through flushed cheeks. She was unable to speak, but instead stared into the giant clear pupil. Though lifeless, the lens emanated force. *But how?*

"Yes," smiled Lias. "You like."

"It is like nothing ... *nothing* else." She reached up her hand to the glass, as if to feel a glow. The lens' height surpassed her own by at least seven feet. "And to think ... when it emits light. This man-made device can be seen for ... for ..."

"Miles," finished Lias.

Evalyn shook her head. The idea of oil, a flame, and prismed glass seen by hundreds, perhaps thousands of weary sailors. Long before they could ever distinguish the confluence of land and make out evidence of Charleston's harbor, they were seeing a light pinprick their darkness. It seemed to her otherworldly. Evalyn remembered the words from the booklet Lias loaned her: "The bending of the light. Light disperses in all directions. The angled prisms in a Fresnel lens refract the light so that it projected outward horizontally in a compressed, intense beam."

"You understand it now, yes?" Lias looked at his children and then at Evalyn.

"No," whispered Evalyn, engrossed, her eyes studying the len's graduating arches and circles. "Uh, yes," she lifted her head and met Lias' confused expression. "Yes, and no. It is just so … overwhelming. And I believe it to be, so far at least, the most fascinating experience of my life." A joyous twitter escaped, and she brought her hand to her mouth.

"Yes! I think so, too! I think so every day I come here," said Lias, grinning. "I never tire of it."

The children, who seemed to be studying the exchange between the adults and simultaneously marveling at the lens, both grabbed at the len's curtain at the same time.

"Papa," said Erik first. "Can we pull, please? We want to see outside."

"Yes. It is soon dusk. In fact, we must look and I must take you down so I can do my job." Lias winked at Erik. "Careful to take curtain along pole, as not to rip."

Erik and Elsa, each gripping a fistful of black linen, stepped aside in the same direction. Revealed was a full 360-degree view through leaded glass.

"Come," said Lias, holding his hand out again to Evalyn, who took it. He led her to a glass door, supported by a metal frame, that – when opened – revealed the parapet, a metal platform and railing that wrapped fully around the outside of the lantern room at the top of the tower. She stepped through the opening and gasped. Lias released her hand and directed his daughter and then son onto the gallery.

Standing at the top of the lighthouse mesmerized Evalyn. A salty breeze fluttered her hair and skirt. While she thought less of God than she knew she should, the reality of two words, "I Am," struck her.

Though nothing tangible moved her body, she still grasped the metal railing as she stared. The creator's power was made evident, clearer than ever before, in the peering down at spacious marsh plains marrying pine forests to her left and an endless void of water to her right.

Sea birds flew below, not above.

Lias reached inside the door and picked up a telescope, which grew long as he extended section after section. "This is how I see. You want to see?" He leaned down to Elsa and positioned her hands to help him hold the device. "Close one eye; look with other." After some adjusting, Elsa said, "Oh, Papa! I see ship! Look!"

"Please, me!" insisted Erik.

First, Lias took the telescope and fixated on the horizon. "Yes. That is Aurora, I believe. She is returning to her Charleston home." He handed the telescope to Erik.

"Careful. It must not fall to the ground. Very costly!"

When Erik finished with the telescope, he offered it to his teacher.

Evalyn struggled clumsily with the device. In her attempt to focus, she pulled her head back from the eye piece and toward it several time before she felt Lias' fullness behind her. He wrapped around her small frame to grip the telescope and steady it. "Now, look." She quivered slightly and then focused on the enlarged image in front of her. Trance-like, she scanned the horizon for several seconds. When she drew the telescope away from her eye, Lias stepped back and to her side. "Thank you," she said.

He smiled.

While Lias allowed Elsa and Erik another turn with the telescope, Evalyn stared expressionlessly at the sea. Her face, though, belied an inner churning. Still gripping the railing, she took a step forward on the circular platform. But she glanced back at Lias first, who seemed to read her thoughts. He nodded. She walked along the platform, carefully, drawing in deeper and deeper breaths – as if to absorb the scenes and stuff them into her being so they could be pulled out at whim. She desired not to leave the place. Each step was a different view, of earth and sky and clouds and beauty. Purest beauty.

On the marsh side of the lighthouse, Evalyn dared to look down again. Perhaps it was the open platform and fresh air, but her stomach did not lurch. She scanned the grounds around the home. Barely discernible from the elevated perch appeared the ant-size figure of Agnes. Her head was cocked back, her hand just above her eyes in a shielding salute. She was staring upwards. Evalyn startled and stepped back against the tower's glass, as if doing so would hide her from view. She hurriedly finished her gallery stroll.

"We must go now," announced Lias. "We must descend."

THE WIFE

"You give to store, with money. You bring change." Agnes thrust a piece of paper and some coins in Evalyn's direction one Friday afternoon in late March as she exited the home with her bag.

Daily the weather was beginning to warm by noon. Soon, all-day agreeable warmth would advance toward sweltering heat. At least part of early spring schooling days were spent out of doors. Evalyn planned for the schedule to continue through what she hoped would be a long spring, at least until the three could no longer tolerate summer's mid-to-late afternoon broil. She wondered how the Larssons would fair during their first South Carolina summer.

Evalyn took the money and piece of paper from Agnes, uttered a confused, "Yes, … ma'am," and waited for at least a thank you from her employer. Agnes nodded stiffly and returned inside the home.

Evalyn made her way along the walkway toward the dock to await the skiff that would take her back to James Island.

"Wait!" called Lias.

"I have given list and money!" said Agnes, her hands ringing the apron affixed to her skirt as she reappeared outside the home.

"There is something I wish to add," responded Lias, without looking back at his wife. "Please allow me write another item on her list," he said to Evalyn. She reached into a pocket where she had just deposited the piece of paper and unfolded it. Lias bent down, using his thigh to steady the paper. As he wrote, he explained, "I have been trying to learn what you teach children ... to understand what they tell me evenings. I wish to have journal to write my study and observances ... of the island, too. You may choose which one for me. Yes?" He smiled at her as he refolded the paper and handed it back to her. Words of encouragement formed, a response to his enthusiasm, but she stifled them when she realized Agnes advanced. Evalyn watched over Lias' shoulder as Agnes marched quickly toward them, her arms swinging wildly by her side.

"What is added?" asked Agnes, when she reached them, her voice like a sandpiper's shrill.

As she reached out to snatch the paper from Evalyn's folded hands, Lias grabbed gently his wife's forearm and turned her back toward their home. "Safe journey," he called after Evalyn, who heard the sound of stern but controlled Swedish words drift farther into the breeze as the couple disappeared into the house.

The children's sweet, concerned faces peered down at her from an upstairs window.

Three months, and Evalyn was no closer to understanding or relating to their mother. Agnes was as distant and capricious as Lias and the children were relational and harmonious. Evalyn relied on the latter as she did the tides. But Agnes seemed to her to be born of the ever-changing sea – glass-like to tempestuous with little to know warning.

Lately, muffled quarreling rose up through the joists and floorboards and jabbed at her while she tried to sleep. The Monday evening prior, both she and the children endured a morning of glowering stares and venomous prodding. They stayed silent, intent on the schoolwork, but Agnes seemed at odds with herself and her surroundings, slamming the teapot on the woodstove and kicking at the cat when it tried to enter through the cracked door.

At noon dinner, Evalyn feigned a headache and asked to lie down for a few moments. From her room, with a window view of the lighthouse door, she watched the children run to their father and embrace him as he exited. Elsa seemed to have cried for a moment into her father's overall bib. Lias then squatted in front of his children and listened intently. His expression grave, he entered the home with them trailing cautiously behind.

"Go wash," he instructed Elsa and Erik while looking around the entryway and dining room for his wife. He found her sitting on a bench in the back kitchen area, her body slumped and her shoulders pulsating as a result of convulsive sobs. Lias stood erect, staring out the window to the marshes beyond, but he stroked his wife's hair and pulled her apron-hidden face toward his mid-section. He spoke impassively to her.

Later, after dinner was cleared and the classroom moved down the shore to a graveyard of twisted, wind-smoothed trees, Erik spoke. "Mama is sick," he said in the middle of a lesson on Charleston's British origins.

"What do you mean?"

"Her head. It is sick." He continued to write notes about the lesson as he spoke.

"I think so, too," answered Elsa, who started to cry.

Erik stopped writing and grabbed his sister's hand. In a gesture Evalyn envied, he pulled her close, whispered to her, and used his shirt sleeve to wipe away tears. "She sees … she thinks she sees … things," he said, matter-of-factly. "She told Papa of eyes in the silver watching her. It is only her reflec ... what is word?"

"Reflection."

"Yes. Reflection. Mama said we need to tie the forks and knives and spoons to strings and hang them in trees in the woods so they can watch animals and not her."

******

April 25th was Easter Sunday. The Larssons planned to attend James Island Episcopal. It was to be their first public appearance "in town" – and Lias surprised Agnes with news that they would travel onto Charleston Sunday afternoon to spend an evening and a morning before returning to Morris Island on Monday. An assistant keeper apprentice, Charlie Simms, from Georgetown, was to rotate to Morris Island for a few days, just in time to keep house during the family's short stint away. Lias learned Simms was in training and touring lighthouses on the Carolinas' coast. Lias warned his family that if the weather changed drastically, the trip to town would be cancelled. Ships trumped recognition of Christ's resurrection. But Lias predicted mild conditions would continue through the holiday weekend.

Elsa was excited to wear a new dress. The list given to Evalyn the end of March included pale blue cotton material and white satin ribbon. Agnes' own dress, which she made of a navy fabric, conveyed a fuller skirt and slight Bertha neckline, yet the design complemented her daughter's.

Agnes' spirits appeared lifted as she busied herself with pinning, sewing, and fitting the dresses, letting out the cuff hem of Erik's one pair of dress trousers, and pressing carefully the collars and seams of each item of clothing. During their short breaks from schoolwork, Agnes also asked the children to work castor oil into their leather shoes until a perceptible shine appeared. She trimmed her family's hair and clipped the split ends off her own – even though it would be gathered into a reverent bun.

Nothing more was mentioned about watchful eyes.

Evalyn noted that prolonged isolation was, perhaps, not a friend to Agnes. Her rudder seemed momentarily stabilized at just the anticipation of a change of scenery and interaction with others. Agnes' eager mood caught Evalyn by surprise the Friday morning prior to Easter Sunday.

"This for you," said Agnes, cutting off Evalyn in mid-sentence during a grammar lesson. She placed a delicately fashioned cross, made from leftover fabric scraps with a coordinating crocheted attachment, on the table next to where Evalyn sat. "For Easter," she said, smiling warmly. "To mark place in book."

Evalyn picked up the cross and held it splayed in her palm. The crocheted section, to lie flat on a marked page, hung between her thumb and forefinger. "It is so beautiful," she said, looking up at Agnes, who was still smiling. It was the only truly kind gesture from her employer in more than three months. "I am so thankful."

Stunning Evalyn further, Agnes pulled out the chair next to her and announced, "I learn today. You teach and I listen."

Erik and Elsa stared at their mother.

"Go on ... teach please."

Evalyn resumed and the children's chalk, which hung suspended momentarily as they calculated their mother's actions, lowered slowly. They began again to make scratching sounds on slates in response to Evalyn's questions: "What are three prepositions for place?" She waited for their hands to stop moving. "Elsa?"

"In, on, at."

"Very good. Write a sentence using one or all of them."

Evalyn watched them erase their slates with a piece of rag. "Erik, speak an example to me."

"Papa is *in* the lighthouse."

"Good. Now you write a different sentence and I will check both your slates."

"Bird *on* lighthouse," interrupted Agnes. "This correct, yes?" Her childlike expression waited eagerly for Evalyn's approval.

"Yes. Correct," said Evalyn, letting the verb slide.

Agnes beamed.

Just as quickly as she sat down, she was up again, pushing in her chair forcefully and exiting the room.

Evalyn discerned a furtive glance between siblings before they resumed writing on their slates.

The rest of the morning was spent discerning how salt can be separated from water as well as understanding why a human body cannot survive by drinking salt water. The week previous, Evalyn asked Lias for the use of two tin pails. In one, she had the children collect an inch worth of sea water; the other they filled halfway. Each day, their task was to monitor and record the rate of evaporation in the two pails using a wooden measuring stick. Evalyn anticipated her students' faces when they discovered the water gone and a residue of salt remaining. A few cloudy days had slowed progress, and moisture remained in both pails.

"If we find salt one day, can we use on food?" asked Erik.

"Of course."

Always, Evalyn wove a greater meaning into their lessons, sharing the metaphors for salt as communicated in scripture. Elsa, constantly eager to express her knowledge, followed Erik's question with memorization: "Have salt among yourselves, and be at peace with one another. Matt ..., I mean, Mark 9 and 50."

"Just 9:50 will do ... with the colon in between the chapter and the scripture verse," said Evalyn, smiling. "Well done." She enjoyed the placid but ongoing sibling rivalry and realized that Elsa reminded her of herself.

"What do you think that means ... to have salt among yourselves?" she asked the children.

"To be happy to have salt for food?" asked Erik. "Some food is no good without salt."

"Perhaps. Think a little more."

Erik and Elsa stared blankly at her.

She added: "Salt is good for food, yes. Our words, our actions, our thoughts toward each other need to be like salt … good."

They nodded, allowing the lesson to sink in.

"I want to try our salt," said Elsa, smiling. "I think I will enjoy it very much. And I plan to give some to Mama. It will be good for her, yes?"

"Yes," answered Evalyn, wondering if the deeper meaning eluded them altogether, or if they understood more than she realized.

When they returned to the indoors, the noon-day meal was ready. Agnes served and ate pensively. Her earlier benevolence showed nowhere on her countenance. Lias questioned the children about the salt experiment and Elsa recited again the scripture. Evalyn studied Agnes bemusedly, as she had done over many months.

Upon completing her after-dinner toilette, Evalyn planned to close the week's teaching by having her students re-teach her key aspects of previous lessons. It was a suggestion she read the prior weekend in the education column of the Charleston newspaper. But when she descended the stairs, Agnes waited at the bottom. "You pack up. No more school. Children get ready for Easter Sunday." Then she turned and left Evalyn standing on the bottom stair.

Taken aback, Evalyn returned to her room to pack belongings. She did not know why she was surprised by Agnes' abruptness. Evalyn had come to expect her employer's vacillating nature, but the earlier gesture of the gift followed by a momentary awareness of the English lesson was a disquieting gale. Evalyn decided she would rather not have the candle lit at all than to see it extinguished callously, and with no sensible explanation.

Since she was dismissed earlier than usual, Evalyn packed slowly, expressed to the children and Agnes that she would most likely see them at the James Island Easter picnic, and walked to the boat dock to wait long and impatiently for the skiff. Evalyn assumed Lias, inside the lighthouse, was unaware of her early dismissal. She reflected on her months of teaching, weighing on a thoughtful chart the benefits against the challenges. She sat on a bench watching a small clearnose skate flap its fins against the dock pilings; the many days of lessons swirled in her mind. The children had achieved much, and Lias verbalized almost daily appreciation. The pay was good; she was saving most of her earnings as there were few expenses, except for transportation to and from Morris Island and some props and supplies she purchased as teaching aids. The job's only drawback – the singular frustration, irritation even – was Agnes. For the first time, Evalyn considered that perhaps Agnes never wanted to hire her as a teacher in the first place. *Was it all Lias? Is she jealous? Is it really so important to understand her? To gain her respect? Is her turbulent heart penetrable?*

"What does it matter?" Evalyn asked out loud to no one but the skate and a great blue heron intent on snatching a few fiddler crabs. "I just need to do my job. I'm not here to make friends."

After chastising herself, Evalyn steeled her resolve. Shielding her eyes from the late afternoon sun, she searched the grassy horizon for signs of the skiff, knowing that its captain would arrive only when he was supposed to. Eventually, she succumbed to the sun's warmth. Still keeping a straight back on the bench and her hands folded in her lap, she lulled to short bouts of dozing.

The small vessel's captain arrived on time, as he had every Friday for three months. His dark, sunbaked, leathery hands reached for her bag and, after she settled on the single board seat, he turned gracefully the tiny boat away from the watchful lighthouse.

The skiff captain's predictable silence allowed more room in Evalyn's musings to consider the holiday ahead. Easter and Christmas were the only times her mother truly put down needle and thread to celebrate with others. Though not particularly religious, her mother and stepfather knew that to be absent during these bi-annual Christ-centered holidays was sacrilege to wary neighbors. Society, even at their level, dictated they be seen in church and at the after-gatherings in the small James Island town.

In Charleston, Easter was much more of a social occasion than a religious one, even though all the churches were filled: First Scots Pres, St. Johns, St. Mary's, St. Michael's. Charleston was the city of steeples. But those who managed to hold onto or buy back from Northerners (the ultimate humiliation) their grand homes after losing the war desired to show them during any occasion, especially holidays. Sure, they would go to church first. But then they opened their dining rooms and set the table with ancestral china and silver, at one time hidden from those "damned Yankees." And in Charleston pilau was served on special occasions to remind former planter families that there was once a gilded era when the main staple at not just feasts but nightly suppers had been slave-cultivated rice.

Most James Islanders could not afford rice, even for Easter, but they enjoyed canned corn, or milled grits, or pone, or whatever anyone brought to Easter picnics to share. Men presented slow-roasted pigs or an oyster stew; women brought forth proudly their best dishes made with preserved harvests from the previous year. White and black – though not together – anticipated enthusiastically their annual Easter picnics. And, while the Easter service was a reminder of the gospel's resurrection message, the picnic gathering served to catch folks up with one another – and for ladies to sport new fashions.

While at Mac's Mercantile one Saturday fetching goods for the Larssons, Evalyn had ordered with a portion of her wages a bolt of pale violet cloth and a few yards of dark purple, almost black, wide satin ribbon. She planned to spend her Saturday sewing a bustled skirt. Her shirt would be of the whitest cotton, high neck with a slight ruffle. Pretty, but practical as to her station. She was not to pomp about, holiday or not. She was an unmarried working girl. Still, she desired a new dress in which to attend church and community picnics. The dress was mostly completed the weekend previous, but Evalyn planned to add a few delicate touches, after her mother's mandated chore list and after pinpointing lessons for the upcoming week.

"There's quite the hubbub," said her stepfather, mouth full of a roast chicken leg, when she entered during their Friday evening supper, which took place later as the days lengthened. He did not stand as a gesture of politeness. Instead, he looked up indifferently and took another bite.

"What do you mean?" asked Evalyn, already annoyed after just moments over the threshold of her home.

"Hubbub about your employers planning to show themselves this weekend. Much speculation about 'em since no one's really laid eyes on 'em since they cast themselves onto Morris. Guess we'll learn if Swedes have two heads or one." He chuckled.

"You will find them perfectly normal." A momentary image flashed of twirling cutlery hanging from trees.

"I hope we can meet them, properly," said her mother, acknowledging her husband instead of Evalyn. "All these months of my daughter leaving us to work with strangers … Isn't right."

"I would hope that by now you would be proud …"

"That you leave me every week to do all the work here, alone? And then you come back on Friday only to act like sewing is beneath you."

"It's not beneath me," said Evalyn, fatigued from the weight of her mother's divergent nature. "I simply prefer teaching. It's my gift … a blessing. I wish, for goodness sake, you would understand that."

"Don't you dare speak profanely in this house …" said her stepfather.

"… especially at the start of Easter, no less," her mother continued.

Evalyn wanted to shout, "Truly!" in an overtly sarcastic tone. She yearned to stomp her feet and slam her fists on the table. But she picked up her plate and announced sedately, "I will take my supper in my room and unpack. Good night."

******

Evalyn remembered as a little girl meeting in homes for church services as all the island's founding denominations' buildings were burned during the war. By early 1870s, James Island Presbyterian had a new cypress-board building, which by 1886 had been expanded to accommodate a growing congregation. But the Easter Sunday sermon that April morning seemed the same, verbatim, as those in Evalyn's childhood. She awoke anticipating the dry message, so she read the first chapter of John before dressing in her room. Always it awed her spiritual senses, revealing the true and overwhelmingly powerful reason for Christ's death on a cross.

During the church service, her mind wandered to those passages in John, and then she diverted to considering the Larssons at the community picnic. What would be their countenance toward her in public? How would Agnes handle James Islanders' curious stares? How would the children acknowledge her?

Erik and Elsa, comfortable and carefree while on their beach jaunts far from their home, expressed moments of unreserved fondness for their teacher. A momentary holding of her hand. A leaning in, while showing a shell or some other treasure. Sitting closely.

Evalyn trusted that their actions and expressions on Easter Sunday would suggest to James Islanders only parental loyalty and stoicism – the same mask they donned when returning to their mother after an outdoor lesson on Morris Island. She expected the children's attachment to her would not be revealed outwardly. Playing over and over in the foreground of her mind was an expected and respectful scene of the Larssons in unison greeting her, "Happy Easter to you, Miss Gray," and her return salutation, "Thank you, family; a Happy Easter to you as well."

Listening to the cheerful orchestra of bird songs and distant rooster crows, peering down to hands folded in the lap of her new and freshly pressed dress, and feeling warming sun beams penetrating through stained glass – Evalyn felt that all conspired toward a glorious spring day.

But it was not to be.

When Evalyn traveled after church with her parents in their simple carriage to a grassy half acre the McLeods set aside for such gatherings as holiday picnics, there was already a significant crowd. Plentitude quilts were spread like patterned garden plots in rows and around the outer edges of the designated land. In the center was a line of tables covered in mismatched linens; Evalyn remembered Samuel saying that the negroes pulled tables from the McLeod family's surplus storage shed for such events. She hoped to actually see him while at McLeod's, but she doubted such a meeting. He would be celebrating with his own family and friends along the banks of Wappoo Creek, far out of sight of the white assembly. White and black worlds, though close in proximity, were often miles apart, especially during social gatherings. Easter picnicking menus might even parallel in some respects – cold fried chicken, cooked earlier that morning or the night before, potato salad, and hoppin' john. But the black families, lamented Evalyn, also enjoyed fried, delectable "peelers," molting crabs that could be eaten, soft shell and all. Samuel gave her a taste when she was younger. Her culinary senses had delighted at once in the crunchy and plump crustacean. But her family and other whites she knew considered soft shell crabs black cuisine. The culinary taboo confused Evalyn, especially since it was acceptable for white families to enjoy eating the meat of the same type of crab when its shell was hard.

And then all James Islanders, white or black, enjoyed at picnics boiled and fried shrimp, served with a preserved chow-chow made from the previous summer's bounty, as well as cat-head biscuits dripping with local honey and hand-spun butter.

Evalyn's stomach flickered a subtle hunger pang. She had eaten little in anticipation of the Easter picnic feast. She hoped one of the reverends called a prayer sooner than later so that children, then women, and then men could line up to help themselves to a sampling of myriad dishes added to the tables.

She first noticed Thomas and his wife, who exhibited a bump on which she rested tellingly both her hands. The sight failed to affect Evalyn. Instead, she scanned quickly past them to an official-looking throng crowded around her employers. Lias' expression mirrored that of his two offspring: bright, attentive, curious, enamored. The children seemed to her quivering foals ready to run free. Agnes, in her starched, newly sewn raiment, including a too-tightly-tied bonnet bow, exaggerated an already protruding and severe chin.

Activity fluttered around the blond family. Evalyn watched Lias extend his hand over and over again; Agnes forced a smile toward the inquisitive faces. The more people gathered to say hello and to introduce themselves to the "intrestin' and foren'" lighthouse family, the more Agnes shrunk beside and then behind her husband. Now and then, Evalyn saw Agnes muster a brightening in her spirit, but it withered before it had a chance to adhere.

Evalyn felt like she missed her chance to greet them. She decided to wait until the crowds' ardor eased.

And then Evalyn witnessed a darkening, like a solar eclipse, clouding Agnes' light gray eyes. From her vantage point, Evalyn could see Agnes' grip tighten around her husband's arm. Evalyn was doubtless that picnickers noticed fear clearly manifesting in Agnes, but her family seemed oblivious to her rising unease. They were swept on a wave of admiration.

Evalyn thought later that she must have been the only one to see the massive white boar, its fowl jowls and testicles flapping in unison as it ran, heading toward the assemblage. Two tick hounds, seemingly insensible to the humans gathered, pursued the escaped pig closely. To Evalyn's recollection, it should have happened so fast, yet the scene was an excruciatingly slow occurrence, giving her time to absorb shocking details. The pig, apparently more fearful of the gaining canines than the humans, charged forward. Once aware, the crowd responded quickly to the snorting mass invading them; individuals jumped and skirted about to give the creature a wide berth. Evalyn, shock still, became part of the chaotic landscape. The Larssons, however, seemed not to understand the commotion until it was upon them. With his muscular forearm, Lias instinctively swept his children to one side. But in his distraction greeting islanders, he failed to sense his wife's position behind him. He stepped back and turned, looking for her, and in doing so knocked her to the ground at the same time the pig and the dogs were upon them. The hulking male swine pressed heavily and cruelly upon the frame of Agnes, soiling her dress and contorting her bonnet. The animals ran on, but they left behind more chaos.

For a moment, barely long enough for a breath, it seemed all of James Island froze. It was but a speck in the lives of those in attendance, but one that would invade their consciousness until death — an unfathomable flash to be talked about and pondered over for generations.

Lias moved first, squatting to inspect his stunned wife. "Is she dead?" someone nearest Evalyn whispered. It was a fair question, for Agnes appeared ready for burial, rigid, with arms to her side, palms up, and eyes staring widely toward the heavens. Lias inspected her, feeling her arms and legs, all the while asking of her condition. She remained silent, shocked mute. He took a handkerchief from his pocket and wiped away dirt and blood on her forehead and cheek, violated by the animal's cloven hooves. The fleetingly silent onlookers murmured concerns, but their dissertations rose steadily as more voices joined.

It was when Lias slid his hand behind her back and gently implored her to sit up that Agnes seemed — as one in attendance described — as if the very demon that occupied the pig rented space inside her body. Her body's rigidity gave way to a convulsing forward motion. She half sat up and then rolled to one side, pausing on all fours. "Agnes, let me help ..." said Lias, grabbing at her arm in an attempt to steady her; his attempt at aid elicited from her a prolonged scream incomparable to any sound familiar to present-day ears. The scream transitioned into a high-pitched moan and finally tapered off before exiting Agnes. Still on all fours, she waved her right arm wildly as if his touch burned her flesh. Evalyn noticed all traces of Lias' earlier sanguine demeanor flee his countenance.

"No! No! No!" she shouted, lifting herself to a standing position. She glared, hollow-eyed, at and through the dazed onlookers. Elsa and Erik had taken a few steps back in an attempt to distance themselves from the disturbing scene.

"Dear … let me …," Lias attempted again, picking up her bonnet and reaching out his hand, which she smacked away.

"I am well! I am well!" she yelled in English, smearing the blood and dirt with the back of her hand so that it formed a pinkish paste across her facial features. She mumbled in Swedish, grabbed the crumpled, soiled bonnet and affixed it to her head; clumps of dirty hair poked haphazardly from beneath ruffles. "Ve eat, yes?"

Evalyn gasped and heard others' gasps rise around her. *She must be in shock.*

Agnes staggered to the tables of food, a dirty hand reaching for a plate. Beyond Agnes, in close range of her, Evalyn noticed her mother and stepfather for the first time since the ordeal began. Her mother's eyes mirrored the sentiments of the surrounding masses: naked disgust.

Before Evalyn realized what she was doing, she moved toward Agnes in a few bounding steps. She blocked her from contaminating a basket of cutlery. Mustering a soothing voice, she offered, "Mrs. Larsson, I am so sorry you have had such a fright. Please accompany me to where you can get cleaned up good as …"

The blow whirled Evalyn full around. Before turning back to face Agnes, Evalyn touched at her split lip and tasted immediately metallic salt. Covering her mouth and righting herself, Evalyn was confronted by Lias' sharp, but sympathetic face. His massive arms encircled swiftly his distraught wife and guided her forcibly away from the picnic. All the while, Agnes hurled at her husband an unintelligible stream of Swedish rants.

The elderly Mrs. Blakenship, a Civil War widow, stepped forward to assist Evalyn, handing her a handkerchief. Evalyn tried to thank her, but the words failed to form around the puffing lip. At once,

Evalyn's mother, never the nurse-made type, was beside her, arm looped just under the elbow. She took the handkerchief from Evalyn's shaking hand and pressed it maternally against her daughter's mouth while at the same time leading her in the opposite direction of the Larssons.

Elsa and Erik, visibly disgraced to their cores, tried to keep their backs turned from James Islanders; they slinked toward the feign and pony pulled up to drive them back to the marsh dock, where a skiff would exile them back to Morris Island.

******

These shores are haunted by madness, thought Evalyn.

A week away from the Easter Sunday lunacy, she stared through her window on Morris Island at the shoreline below. The unease in her spirit caused her to reflect on unpleasantries, principally her mother and stepfather's immediate assumption she would quit her job. "She's mad!" they expressed in every way, refined and rudely.

Evalyn considered their plea. Agnes' behavior was certainly unlike anything she – or others – had witnessed before. She pondered the Easter scene until its details became an elaborate etching on her mind. Until Easter, Evalyn had thought of Agnes as an insecure soul;

jealous, perhaps, of her relationship with the children. Or, maybe bitter about the family's move to America. Aloof, conceivably, because of the language difficulty. Evalyn considered that her odd tendencies could even have been brought on by island isolation.

But Easter's event illuminated a deeper state. Agnes' mental instability glowered unmistakably.

Fixating on some breaking waves and the lowering sun, Evalyn recalled her parents' flabbergasted expressions when she told them she would return to Morris Island. She knew that most James Islanders were talking about Agnes, as well as weighing in on her career as lighthouse teacher. Whispers and stares were conspicuous as she shopped Mac's for supplies or made deliveries of sewn goods to her mother's clients.

And as she stepped back into her other-worldly role as teacher on a lighthouse island, a particular history module bobbed to mind: one taught to the children weeks earlier. Lias had requested they understand the war. Evalyn had obliged, but her version was censored and weighed.

Diverting thoughts dissolved and she noted again the shoreline, *haunted by madness.*

Yes, she had shared select first-hand accounts from William Gilmore Simms and Mary Chestnut. She taught the children how and why Union and Confederate soldiers a little over 20 years earlier died on the same shores where they now learned and played. What she did not tell them was how many of those soldiers' blood, from gut wounds, shattered skulls, and missing limbs, saturated their island. Evalyn explained that the war was mostly about freeing enslaved people, but she left out how Charleston had been the destination for thousands of unfortunate souls tormented while crossing the vast Atlantic, chained to death and suffocated by stench, succumbed to insanity. Before entering Charleston's port, "damaged goods" were hurled into the undertow; their rotting flesh had permeated the sandy fibers of the island's foundation.

These shores are tainted by madness.

She trembled, picturing again Agnes' rigged body … the scream … the hand coming toward her face.

"Miss Gray."

Evalyn startled, knocking a lesson book off a table by the window.

"I am sorry. I did not want to frighten …" Lias stood before her, his bell-top cap tight to his chest. It was the first time he had crossed the threshold to her room – the first time up the flights of stairs to speak to her.

No one had greeted her earlier at the docks. Relieved, she had walked hastily down the boardwalk and into the home, scurrying up the stairs to her bedroom without acknowledging the subdued voices emanating from the dining room. During the week prior, she tried to imagine myriad scenarios. It would have been easier to quit and avoid forever the Larsson ignominy.

"I … she, Mrs. Larsson, asked me to speak to you." Ordinarily stalwart and bulky, Lias stood before Evalyn a depleted man. He glanced back at the open door as if checking for Agnes' presence. "She understands if you not want to be here … if you have hatred for her. She is sorry for behavior." He said this loudly, glancing again at the door.

"I … she … my job …" tried Evalyn. What she wanted to say, but was flummoxed beyond articulation, was that what happened within their personal lives as a family would not affect her teaching. When he took a few more steps toward her, checking once more that no one had quietly materialized at the doorway, the air in the room instantly thickened and Evalyn felt a flush upon her chest that eased up her neck and onto her otherwise pale cheeks.

Lias leaned toward her and whispered, "She *feels* darkness."

"I'm sorry?" quivered Evalyn, noticing a slight trembling in her legs.

"She *feels* darkness. She *knows* it. I have seen this happen with her before … in Sweden. I think coming here, a nice change … beautiful America and southern coast is all I read in a lighthouse journal. She is not bad woman. She is …scared, of darkness in her mind." He brought two fingers to his brow.

"I am sorry I send word for you to stay away from us for one week. We needed time …," he trailed off.

Evalyn read foreboding on his shoulders, which slumped slightly. He continued, "But we need you here, too … the children. You are a … how do you say? Wall?"

"Buffer?"

"Yes, I think … maybe. God, his word, it teaches us … I read, light shines in darkness. Yes? You are some light for children … for me, uh, for us. I think." He managed a somber smile. "It was very bad in Sweden. I cannot tell you … I seek her some help, but it is difficult. A doctor for the mind, he does not understand her darkness. He is not with us when she does things that are … um … unexplainable."

His fingers twisted the brim of his cap and he looked down. "I am so angry inside that she has hit you. I am sorry."

Slowly, dreamlike, Evalyn reached out her hand and rested lightly her four fingers on his forearm. Both drew in breath. Lias raised his head, and their gaze settled on one another; lingering. So much about a marriage and turmoil and need expressed in a moment.

The implications of that simple, empathetic touch would reverberate through the ages.

Evalyn withdrew first, and Lias took a step back, flexing his forearm as if to fortify his skin from further sensation.

"I … uh … oh, please know that I forgive her," said Evalyn, disrupting the unease. "Please tell her that. I know that she may not want me to speak of it to her directly."

"No, she will not. And thank you. You are kind to forgive."

"And I do desire to continue teaching. The children … they are such eager students and have learned much."

"Thank you. Yes. They need you here. We ...," again his voice trailed. Unable to find words, he turned to leave.

"What can I do?" asked Evalyn, in a too desperate tone she hoped he did not detect. "I do not want to intrude, but if there is anything, anything at all I can do to help you – or a different way to be around her, please tell me. I always think she is displeased with me and I try to avoid interaction, but if I should speak to her more ..."

"No." He turned slightly but did not face her. "You keep teaching children, please. I will ... see to Mrs. Larsson." He took a few steps toward the stairwell, but then paused as if remembering something. Then he turned and walked back toward her. Again, she flushed warm. He leaned into her left side and in a low voice said, "I am ... sorry I not tell you of her ... um, of her problems when you first come here to teach. I hope it happens no more. Please ... you must tell me if the darkness is clear to you, when I am working in the lighthouse ... Please, if she ... if she frightens you or the children with her ways. You must tell me. She may become worse, now that ..." He paused. "*Please*. You tell me. Yes?"

"Yes."

It was not until he left her room and descended the stairs that Evalyn felt herself breath again.

THE SUSPICIONS

Soggy grayish taupe sand imprinted with small footprints. Evalyn allowed the children to remove their shoes when they could no longer see the house and only the mid-section to the top of the lighthouse peered at them over the island trees. They were too far beyond the house for Agnes to see their folly. And Evalyn thought that even if Lias viewed them through telescope from his lofty perch, he would not mind.

They needed this. They needed freedom from the scattered closet of their mother's mind. They needed to know their teacher remained a consistent, committed force. They needed to be children.

Outwardly, except for Lias' apology, all had continued on Morris Island as if Easter never happened. Evalyn was certain the holiday might for a lifetime rear ugly and unsettling in the children's thoughts – not as recognition of Christ's victory over death and a celebration for the spiritually minded, but as family ignominy of the worst kind.

Lias. His exposed and vulnerable state days before infiltrated her thoughts. That twinge, unexpected and uninvited, just by his presence in her room, nagged troublingly. No other man, except for Samuel – not even Thomas – had stirred her womanliness beyond propriety's boundaries.

"Miss Gray?" Elsa interrupted Evalyn's longings.

Evalyn looked into the concerned face and smiled.

"You are fine, yes?"

"Yes!" Evalyn sat on the remains of a tree and unlaced her shoes. She yanked them off and threw them carelessly to the ground.

Elsa's eyes widened.

"You, too?" asked Erik.

"Me too!" she answered.

Elsa's feet sunk deeper into the boggish sand as she grasped her teacher's actions.

Evalyn jumped up from the downed tree and attempted to run, but sandy suction pulled at her feet. She laughed, loud and forceful into a northern breeze sweeping across waves. She exaggerated her movements, marching overextended and in slow motion. Erik laughed and Elsa joined, her downturned mouth opening to release a squeal. Evalyn led the march; her charges fell in behind her as a lean, imaginary army. Evalyn stopped and pointed just a few yards off shore as a porpoise emerged, blew spray from its air hole, and submerged again. The three sunk deeper into sand but held breath with the porpoise. Erik gasped when the animal's gray eyes re-emerged. "31!"

"I counted 29!" said Elsa.

"You count too slowly. It was 31 seconds this time," he insisted.

Evalyn smiled at them. Her spontaneity had worked to assuage, at least temporarily, unsettling thoughts.

"Ahh! I'm stuck!" yelled Elsa.

"No, you are not!" responded Erik, laughing. "You just want me to rescue you! Last one back to dry sand is rotten egg!"

Elsa pulled her feet out of the muck and kicked wet chunks into the air. Giggling, she raced after him. Her light frame glided less encumbered over the thick sand, and she almost reached him before he announced himself the winner. The siblings collapsed near the tree where Evalyn had removed her shoes. She slowly made her way over to the children, enjoying their uninhibited display. As she approached, her eyes moved to a branch overhanging the spot where they sat, panting. Suspended, as if dead by the neck, was a four-foot snakeskin. A slight breeze caused movement and the luminous skin reflected imprints of scales.

"Come away, children," panicked Evalyn, her eyes searching beyond the ominous sight to the other branches and around the tree. They scurried toward her, looking back in fear. "I did not notice," she said pointing, "when I was sitting here earlier. Do you see?"

They nodded their heads, eyes wide.

"Remember what I have taught you? Where there is a snakeskin …"

"There is a snake," finished Erik.

******

The temperate nature of the Larsson household persisted. Evalyn detected in Agnes not even a slight acknowledgement of that inauspicious day. Her cool, detached demeanor endured. She expressed to Evalyn no humility or shame. If anything, she seemed to Evalyn to be more aloof and vacant. Nevertheless, worries of Agnes' lurking or judging ebbed somewhat so that Evalyn concentrated wholly on teaching.

After Evalyn returned on Friday to James Island, at the close of her first week back teaching post-Easter, she was able to shrug off prying curiosity.

"It was temporary mania, nothing more," Evalyn told her mother, stepfather, and others. "She was already nervous about what people would think of her and her dress, and the pig startled her into hysteria. It might happen to any of us."

Many nodded in agreement, but then articulated within the safety of quiet homes and bonded families that Agnes Larsson's episode was way more than apprehension. What they all witnessed was akin to Luke's Legion; yet, instead of an internal demon pouring from a man into a pig herd at Jesus' command, a crazed and scared hog had antagonized an already sprite-possessed woman. Agnes showed them all a severe exacerbation of the kind they would not soon forget.

Evalyn was readying herself after the Sunday noon meal to return to Morris Island when Samuel appeared outside her home. Their childhood friendship, because of her father's affiliation with the McLeod family, did not trump Samuel's blackness. He kept to the middle yard and waited for Evalyn's mother, rocking on the porch with hem in hand, to acknowledge his presence.

"Hello to you. I suspect Miss Gray is home, and I wish to speak to her for a moment," mustered Samuel, politely.

"Wait there, boy," she replied, indifferently. Though islanders upheld few of the stringent racial conventions ritualistic and religious in nearby Charleston, his presence reminded her of a husband lost to a cause from which Samuel and "the other negroes" benefitted.

"Samuel!" said Evalyn, descending the home's few porch steps to meet him in the dirt yard.

"How is my friend?"

Just seeing him brought a wave of peace, but also that unwelcomed twinge.

Evalyn's mother had disappeared inside. But from a chair by a window, she occasioned between stitches to glance outside at her daughter's odd attachment.

"Well, and you? How is it that you have escaped the mines?"

"It is only for today. My mother was ill, but she is better. The owner gave me a few hours leave. I learned that you were here. You are the talk of the town, I understand."

"Me? Or my employer?"

"Well, both. I have heard the story told a baker's dozen different ways."

"It was horrid, indeed, but there is so little to distract here that of course this would be the obsessed topic of conversation."

"You desire to continue teaching out there?"

"Yes. I am making strides. The children, they are speaking English well and they, … well … we are fond of one another."

"And the mother?"

Evalyn drew closer to Samuel so that she could lower her voice. "She is ill, indeed. But I believe … at least the father told me so … that I am needed. My presence there subdues her mania somewhat."

"The father has told you this?"

Warmth flushed her chest. "Yes. She has a history of madness."

"Ev …"

"All is well, Samuel. I am alert to the coiled snake!" She laughed. "Your aunt Fally frightened me to death with all her Gullah wisdom!"

"She had to do something to dampen a young girl's spirit," he returned.

"Samuel, are you studying? Are you close to saving the money needed to attend teaching college?"

"I am – both. I cannot allow the other miners to see me reading, or to hear me talking this way." He laughed. "They would be merciless to this poor negro. But I sneak off sometimes after my shift with the few tattered volumes you gave me. I paid the doctor for my mother's medicine, but I am living paltry to save all I receive. Soon. Hopefully, soon. The college has accepted me, so that is the first step."

"And I am so glad for you."

"When I have the money to start, they will have me."

"I suspect you will make a finer teacher than me one day."

"Ha! You are clearly effective, if the father of your charges has expressed it so. But Ev ..." he stared at her intensely. She looked away from his glower and then back again. His voice lost its cheerful lilt. "Mus tek cyear a de root fa heal de tree."

"English, please!" Evalyn managed a smile, but her expression conveyed anticipation of an ominous declaration.

"Take care of the roots to heal the tree."

"I have no idea what that means, but I will think on it. You just cannot help yourself, can you?

"Gullah wisdom. That, and the Bible. Nothing more is needed in this world."

"Says who?"

"My aunt and God. One in the same!" He smiled wide and Evalyn followed. Samuel was perhaps the only person in her life who knew implicitly how and what to speak to her. Their traits meshed unquestionably. *If only* …

She forced herself not to think on it; nothing would ever change the plain fact that he was not white and she was not black. Impossibility and danger quelled any imaginable desire.

Samuel did not stay long in Evalyn's yard. But before he left her, he offered again caution. "Wise as a serpent, gentle as a dove."

"Yes, sir."

******

Spring storms came late to the sea islands in 1886. Farmers lamented the latent water source for crops, but Lias thanked God for calm days. Since his lighthouse posting in December, the seas had shown only mild irritation. Day after day, he logged the weather. He journaled meticulously about the days' activities – every detail. Temperature late March through May stayed pleasantly in the 70s to

80s. Ships entered and exited the harbor day and night, with little in the way of tumultuousness to impede their purpose.

He kept plenty busy maintaining the lighthouse, pristine and at the ready. He trimmed the wick, cleaned and polished the Fresnel lens, and shined the brass frame, and he kept the windows of the len's room so clean that it was often difficult to imagine a solid object was between him and the ocean beyond. He swept and sanitized the lighthouse privy. And, since no ships or boats had yet to need his services, he directed extra time off to such tasks as repainting areas not painted since the original coats were applied when the existing lighthouse was completed 10 years earlier.

Some afternoons, he completed promptly all necessary tasks so he could join the children and their teacher for a science lesson farther down the shore. He was careful to steal away when he knew Agnes to be around the far side of the home hanging laundry, gardening, or setting crab traps by the dock. Agnes did not understand her husband's longing to learn. Routine and a mastery of basic skills were her contentment. Even the lighthouse roused no curiosity in her; Agnes trusted Lias' description of its wondrous anatomy and cared not to see for herself, no matter how many times he proposed enthusiastically a grand tour. She had peeked inside the door and had stood at the base and looked up, but that was all.

Lias attended primary school in Sweden, followed by a lighthouse academy to comprehend navigational and nautical terms, meteorology, and basic mechanics. Yet, he desired more. His mind required nourishment. Lighthouse manuals he read repeatedly. In the Morris Island home, he found on a small pine bookcase leather-bound copies of *Robinson Crusoe* and *Pilgrim's Progress*, which he had already read once through since January, grasping much but not all of his new language. He planned to read the novels again and again until he comprehended every English word. Occasionally, he asked Evalyn to leave him one of the children's schoolbooks so he could delve deeper into a lesson Erik and Elsa had regurgitated during the evening meal.

His insistence on a teacher for the children was partially selfish. He acknowledged this truth internally and in his prayers just shortly after Agnes, not wanting to face Evalyn after the Easter Sunday calamity, demanded an end to the teaching. He refused emphatically her command. Though he had endured a wild tirade in their native tongue, he remained firm.

Lias had exaggerated to Evalyn Agnes' interest in apologizing. True, he had eked something of a repentant statement out of his wife, but he knew it was not wholly heartfelt. Her distinct psychology obstructed proper comprehension and acknowledgement of wrongful actions. Past experience with her manic mind taught him that once fixated on a thought, it was nearly impossible to alter course.

Still, Lias believed Evalyn's presence *was* a buffer, as he had conveyed to her. A jetty to quell an all-out tempest.

Yes, societal boundaries that Easter Sunday had momentarily evaded his wife because of a pig-induced calamity, but generally he knew her to endeavor to maintain propriety, however steely and strange her daily temperament. Hiding on the island away from any other human contact, except family, would not be beneficial for her or the family. Agnes' dark conscience could only grow darker within the uninhibited comforts of family life. Lias had even noticed fraying threads when Evalyn was off the island each weekend. And he noticed, too, Agnes righting herself in anticipation of Evalyn's arrival.

Lias conceded his reasoning as obstinate, regarding a hired teacher, but he also realized how desperately he wanted, needed, Evalyn to remain in their employ – not only to teach the children so that they might earn an even better place in the world than isolation in a lighthouse – but also to instruct him. In a quaking marriage, any knowledge he absorbed both distracted and quieted rising concerns. They all needed a teacher there, at least to put off, for as long as possible, the inevitable – whatever that might be.

One day, Lias caught up to the threesome farther from the lighthouse than they had ventured previously. He passed white-petaled morning glories attached to their creeping vines; almost translucent crabs weaving around the blooms made it seem as if some of the flowers were alive. A short burst of cicada buzzing seemed an alert to other marsh and shore creatures of Lias' encroachment. He called to his children and Evalyn as they ducked into what appeared to be a green cave – a path covered with vines tightly woven. He made his way to the cave path and peered inside.

"Hello, Mr. Larsson," said Evalyn, a bit startled.

"Can I join for a few moments?"

"Of course. Always." Evalyn had gotten used to his curiosity – his random visits to their outdoor classroom. "But it does not go far. We were just looking to see where the covered path ended."

"We study foliage," said Erik.

"We think this is deer shelter," added Elsa, excitedly. "We find … *exkrementer.*"

The children laughed.

"Now, students," scolded Evalyn, a blush rising to her already warm cheeks. She did not look at Lias for his reaction but heard his faint chuckle. Book in hand, she led them down another narrow path, not more than a foot or so wide, bordered by myriad plants and vines. She first identified poison ivy and cautioned father and children against touching the jagged-edged leaves.

"Yes. I have heard talk of this plant," said Lias.

Where there was a stream of light through the wide, open fan palms, she pointed out trumpet vines, false indigo, and swamp rose-mallows. Cane and sweetgrass grew in odd places. The trail wound back toward the sea where the path, instead of covered in dried, decaying leaves, was a coconut-shell-colored mixture of the marsh's pluff mud and the shore's sand. Once back on the dunes, salt hay and sea oats dominated. She required the children to collect a leaf or a stem of each of the native plants studied. They pressed them between the pages of a hand-stitched journal, an indulgence, a gift, she had ordered for each of them through Mac's Mercantile.

Lias loitered over every plant, absorbing details and asking questions. Evalyn answered what she knew and elaborated more after thumbing through a chapter on plants in the science volume, which she carried in a hand-sewn fabric pouch slung around her shoulders and chest.

As the group exited a greenery-cloaked path, they noticed the ground covered in splats of chalky white. Evalyn looked up. Above them, in one of the island's few tall pines, was a substantial nest, at least five feet in circumference and three feet thick of branches and grasses. When a whitish projectile nearly landed on Elsa's head, they all ran a few feet away and, with chins lifted in unison, observed an osprey pair looking down into their nest, tail feathers protruding over the edge of the nest. Evalyn encouraged the children and their father to back farther from the tree so they could better see two tiny, fuzzy heads with mouths outstretched beneath their parents.

"Amazing! Is that right word?" asked Lias.

"That is a good word to describe this scene," said Evalyn. "Do my students agree?"

Erik and Elsa nodded their heads, chins still raised upward.

"I must return," Lias said, after spending about 30 minutes watching the osprey and evaluating plants. "Thank you."

"You are always welcome to this classroom," she smiled.

"We will test you later, Papa," Erik quipped. But then, catching himself, he said, "We will *tell* you later, Papa."

Lias spoke to the children in Swedish, smiling warmly and tousling their hair while he did so. Evalyn was beginning to recognize his private, gentle reminders to them that their mother did not need to know he sometimes joined them.

Lias made his way back along the shore to the lighthouse. He stopped long enough to watch a marsh rat just ahead of him bending over a slight spray of grass to munch on new growth. He looked out at the sea and reflected for a moment on what he had learned. The rhythmic swoosh of the waves as they unfurled on the sand lulled him. He watched a small tern flitter, hover, and then dive. He planned to ask Evalyn how those birds, and large brown pelicans, could propel themselves so quickly from the sea and immediately take flight.

Just before emerging from the protective shroud that was the island's scrubby forest, existing just yards back from the shore's edge, his routine was to pick up an armful of dried wood. The home's fireplace would always need wood in winter, and his justification – if caught – would be that he took a break from the lighthouse in the middle of the day to add to the firewood pile next to the house.

He placed the wood carefully on a pile stacked near the home's back entrance. He opened the door to the home and, feigning thirst, went to the pitcher resting on a cupboard and poured himself a glass of water. He listened, looked around and out the window from the pantry. He walked to the stairwell and called to her. "Agnes." No answer.

Unconcerned, he left the home and walked the short boardwalk to the lighthouse door. *She must be gardening on the other side of the home, or catching crabs at the dock*, he thought. *Better not to disturb her.*

His eyes always needed a few moments to adjust to the darkness of the lighthouse's first floor. He pulled the heavy steel door closed and lifted his foot to bring it down on the first step. Agnes' presence was a shocking thrust against his chest. He stumbled backwards.

"Agnes!"

She sat on the first step and did not respond to his startled cry. In the lighthouse entryway, which became gray the more his eyes adjusted, he realized she held in one open palm a small bird – a red-winged blackbird, he learned later while disposing of it. With her other hand she pulled slowly on its feathers. As his pupil's aperture took in more light from the tall narrow windows above, he saw black feathers lined up neatly on her ivory skirt-covered thigh.

"Agnes, what are you doing?" He spoke to her in Swedish.

No response.

"Dear, are you ill? You frightened me. Did you accidentally kill the bird? Find it? *Why do you sit here in the dark?*"

No response. She continued to stare at the bird in her hand and pull at the feathers.

"Agnes! I demand to know why you sit here!" Lias snatched the bird from her hand; feathers fluttered from the fabric on her dress and disappeared through the slats in the steel step.

"You go to her! I know you go to her! You want her here for you, not for the children!" she spewed in her native language.

"Agnes, dear. I go to learn ... not to her." He reached out to touch her arm and, reminiscent of Easter Sunday, his touch ignited an animalistic sound, something akin to a scream, yet unrecognizable. It was both an injured and an angry sound. She flailed her arms and pushed past him, pulling on the heavy door. She strained to open it.

From behind her he pushed closed the door with one hand; in his other hand, he still held the dead bird. He pressed his body in behind her, keeping her against the door while obscenities, taunts, and accusations streamed into the taciturn space. Lias remained steadfast. After a few moments, he felt his wife's body surrender to her confinement. Dry sobs rose, and he turned her around and held her close. He whispered, "Do not be afraid. I am here. I am not going anywhere. I want to learn. That is all. You must trust me. A teacher here is good for all of us. You must not allow your mind to take you to places that are untrue, unreal."

Agnes' body convulsed for several moments and moans emanated from her, but no tears came. When she quieted, he pulled her from him, opened the door, and led her onto the boardwalk and back to the house. Along the way, Lias dropped the dead bird.

Inside the house, he guided her to their bedroom, filled a basin with water, swiped her hands with goats' milk and lard soap, and washed them. He dried the hands carefully with a towel and used the same towel to wipe softly around her eyes. Childlike, she allowed him to ease her to their bed.

"Rest while the children are out," he instructed her, watching as she complied, lying down on her back, interlacing her fingers, and closing her eyes. As with former episodes, Lias knew that her amnesic mind, upon rest, often veiled sordid details. He hoped she might awaken from a nap with only shadowy details lingering. Over his wife, he prayed silently for the healing of her mind and, if no such outcome was in God's plan, that he could muster fruits of the spirit to bear his wife and their marriage.

Lias returned to where he dropped the bird along the boardwalk; he picked it up again, walked to the edge of the forest, and threw it forcefully. Anyone watching from afar would have wondered what was happening in the mind of the man who turned, stared blankly at the lighthouse, covered his face with both hands, swiped his eyes with the back of his hands, and then walked gravely to the lighthouse and disappeared within.

******

When the rain came, it was at first steady and light. No palm branches swayed. Grackles still antagonized one another from deep within the crown of the palm trees, and the sea held glass-like, revealing only ripples from raindrops.

Evalyn and the children were forced to stay indoors, even though the skies yielded only a half to an inch of rain daily – at first. Agnes teetered unpredictably from obligatory cordiality to quiet resentment, entering and exiting the dining room/classroom multiple times during schooling hours. Evalyn's decisive attempts to involve her in their studies were met with aloofness. But if Evalyn became reticent, Agnes seemed sometimes to take that as a cue to insert herself arbitrarily into the middle of lessons and discussions. And then, just as impetuously as Agnes' thrust her presence into a scene, she recoiled and slunk off – without excuse or explanation.

Lias read incessantly the previous years' logbooks looking for historic patterns. The preceding August produced hurricanes that bore damaging tropical cyclones. Eighteen-eighty-five had been, in fact, a bad year for weather. The former keeper's notes described survivors of capsized boats and damaged ships who were treated in the newly constructed Life Saving Station just up the shore from the lighthouse. The Station was equipped with blankets, bandages, lanterns, and cots enough to house temporarily a dozen men; all items were inventoried and checked regularly by Lias. A boat ramp held a carriage with a surfboat that was oiled and at the ready. The former keeper's notes and narratives would aid him, he thought hopefully, if late summer to autumn weather again proved perilous.

June into July dumped above-average rainfall. Sometimes clouds remained low and released steady, droning showers, while just as many days were pleasant – though windy – in the mornings, and then a menacing blackness invaded and deluged the island with a flood of water through many afternoons into evenings. The lighthouse anemometer measured regular wind speeds of 30 to 50 miles per hour.

During the day, Lias watched the tombstone gray horizon, compared the logbook history with the daily calculations and measurements, and prayed that he would be able to do his job when tested.

Wind and rain exacerbated gradually Agnes' irregular state. She paced, a caged animal. She stopped often at windows, eyes wide, mouth agape, fixated on the weather's exterior effects. Sea myrtles and yaupon growing near the home bent and swayed. Gulls labored against violent air currents. When the summer failed to gift the family with stretches of kind weather, Agnes verbalized concerns during evening meals.

"We are safe," Lias would tell her, but his assurances did nothing to pacify his wife. He feared another episode but acquiesced to an unpredictability he did not have the power to control.

Although the summer weather mysteriously cooperated each Friday and Sunday afternoons just long enough to allow Evalyn safe passage from and to Morris Island, a particularly severe storm lingered until well after dark one Friday in late July. Evalyn, packed and ready, waited for three hours for the storm to abate. She did not want to bear Agnes for a weekend. Despite dread dealings with her mother and stepfather, Evalyn benefitted from her few days off the island each week. But she also hoped that the skiff captain had not ventured into the tidal creek and gotten himself in a precarious state. She could not be certain. He had been taxiing her since January without fail; they had not discussed circumstances that might keep that arrangement from occurring. Around 7 p.m., Lias, soaked and windswept, barged into the home.

"I've come to pack up a bit of supper," he said to Agnes. "I must stay in the light. Bad tonight. Hoping no souls try to reach harbor."

Dripping at the entryway, he glanced at the stairwell and noticed Evalyn standing beside her valise. "Your man will not come," he told her. "And, if he does, you will not go with."

"I am worried …"

"He is smart man. He will not come. You will stay."

Agnes, who had left Lias to gather a basket of food stuffs in the pantry, stopped, turned, and glared at him as he spoke to Evalyn.

"Go," he said, pointing upstairs. "You stay here this evening … perhaps all the weekend."

Lias did not notice the wrath in his wife's gaze, but Evalyn did. As she climbed the stairs, valise in hand, she both felt and saw Agnes' riled stare. By the time Lias turned his attention away from Evalyn, Agnes was in the pantry collecting food and drink.

Evalyn sat on the edge of her bed, hands folded in her lap; her valise remained packed with necessary weekend clothing and toiletries. She stared at the room's wide wall in front of her, the muffled sound of the entryway door opening and closing seeped through pine floors, and then Evalyn guessed the footsteps were of Agnes retreating to her bedroom.

Evalyn examined one of the room's few adornments, a small painting with a gilded frame weathered most likely from old age and saline air. Though the ornamental frame was of fleur-de-lis carvings and wave-like swirls, the painting depicted in three quarters of the scene foamy water crashing on large rocks. The remaining canvas expressed a horizon of burgeoning sun rays emerging from a dissipating storm cloud. The contrast was of turbulence against stone, light upon calm seas.

Her gaze shifted from the painting on the wall to the window, where summer's lingering light allowed Evalyn to view in the distance tumultuous waves crashing not against large rocks, as Atlantic shores had none, but upon flat sandy beaches. They roared in, goliath-like, and then were dragged back to make room for relentless armies of them. Howling wind against the windowpanes and siding, married with the muffled but persistent sound of bellowing waves, disquieted Evalyn at her core. She imagined Agnes beneath her, knees drawn tightly to her chest.

A bolt of lightning and the immediate boom of thunder that pursued it startled Evalyn from her bed perch. She lit her lantern. Late afternoon light still strained in, but Evalyn wanted to brighten the gray, cloud-filtered room, and she decided she would read and plan for the week ahead. *Idle hands* … She would not let the devil get a foothold in her thoughts. She planned to make the best of her weekend encampment on Morris Island – stay in her room until Sunday if necessary.

Evalyn was well into a detailed outline regarding a science lesson on shell identification when Elsa's high-pitched scream caused her pencil to fling from her hand. Before she could get to her door, footsteps were already pounding on the stair treads.

"Miss Gray!" Elsa burst into her room, her delicate face, sheet-white, communicated horror.

"What …"

"Mama …"

Elsa turned and ran back down the stairs with Evalyn following. Elsa rushed into her parents' bedroom, but Evalyn hesitated instinctively. At the threshold, her eyes searched. In the corner was Agnes' crumpled form. Erik rubbed at her back while whispering softly in Swedish. *His father's son*, thought Evalyn.

"She is hurt," said Elsa, who motioned for Evalyn to come over.

"I was taking care ... I did not want Elsa to see," whispered Erik.

It was not until Evalyn drew closer that she saw the blood stains on Agnes' skirt, Erik's shirt, and the floor. Agnes, dazed and weeping, relented while Erik unwrapped a cloth from around her arm. Faint, parallel red lines were stacked up like rungs on a ladder, from just above her wrist almost to the flexor, opposite her elbow. The blood had begun to coagulate closest to her wrist. It still pooled at the edges near the arm's bend. From lifeline to lifeline. A cut at the radial or brachial artery may have ended her, but Agnes' cuts appeared slight, calculated, thought Evalyn.

"Get me two clean towels and a small basin of water," instructed Evalyn of Elsa.

Agnes began speaking slowly, methodically, but in Swedish.

"What is she saying?" Evalyn asked Erik.

"She says she not want to be here. She told her papa she did not want to marry a lighthouse keeper. She wanted to stay at her farm ... away from bright light. It sees all. It sees all. *It sees all* ... Mama! Stop!" Erik tried to deflect his mother's possessed mantra.

Elsa arrived with cloth and water. "Sorry I take long time. I warm it a little."

"Good," said Evalyn, managing a composed smile.

Evalyn cradled Agnes' arm in her lap and began to wipe gently. Agnes flinched and looked up at her. "You take my husband. He tires of me." Tears covered her face.

"No! No, of course not. You must not think such things."

"He tires of my darkness. You are happy. I am sad. He tires of sad."

"He respects me and my skills as a teacher. Nothing more."

"Res ... pect?"

Erik whispered the Swedish word.

"Only respect. You have nothing to fear," said Evalyn.

Erik translated Evalyn's words to his mother.

Mollified, momentarily, Agnes retreated back into a Swedish cadence of regret. Erik translated: "Mor and Far – her mama and papa – they believe she will be better if married. They ... *no Mama*!"

"What is it Erik? I want to know her thoughts," implored Evalyn.

Erik spoke irritatingly to Agnes in Swedish and then continued in English to Evalyn. "She said they forced her to marry Papa. They give him money. He is happy to take her to America, but she not happy. Never happy. She is not ..." Erik stood from his stooped position beside his mother. He glared down at her and left the room.

"Erik!" called Evalyn.

"I will do it," said Elsa, touching Evalyn's arm.

Agnes, trance-like, seemed not to notice Erik's departure. She kept talking, to no one.

"She not want us ... us, children," translated Elsa, tears formed and lingered on her lower lids. "She said she not want us to have her darkness in us like her darkness."

Evalyn finished cleaning and wrapping Agnes' arm and secured the cloth with a hair ribbon. She helped Agnes to her feet. The memory of Agnes' hand smacking against her face entered briefly Evalyn's thoughts. Before her, though, was a woman reduced. She became mute, allowing Evalyn and Elsa to untie and unfasten her outer garment. Undergarments appeared unstained by blood. Elsa took the clothing to a wash basin and submerged it, scrubbing at the blemished areas with a bar of soap. Evalyn removed an almost identical day dress off a wardrobe hook and pulled it over Agnes' head. Agnes stood, still and pliable. Her gray eyes vacant; pupils dilated.

Evalyn led Agnes to the bed. She sat down, and as Evalyn put her hand behind Agnes' back to lower the woman to a lying position, Agnes grabbed Evalyn's arm. Her eyes suddenly became clear and she stared directly into Evalyn's. "I feel ground … move. I feel …" She closed her eyes, released her grip on Evalyn's arm, and allowed herself to be lowered onto the bed.

Evalyn shuddered.

As she turned away, she felt again Agnes' grip. "You are kind … thank you." Agnes closed her eyes for a second time and Evalyn watched as her body succumbed quickly to an exhausted sleep.

Evalyn joined Elsa, who was scrubbing the floor clean of blood. The basin in which she refreshed and wrung the clothing turned a pinkish hue. Elsa looked up at Evalyn. Tears spilled. Evalyn pulled her in close, allowing tears to soak into the shoulder cloth of her blouse.

After thoroughly cleaning all traces of Agnes' cutting, Evalyn met the children in the parlor. Both had changed their clothing.

Cleaned clothing hung drying in the mudroom. Both their faces retained the splotchy redness of sorrow.

"Your Mama is …"

"… mad!" inserted Erik.

"Sick," corrected Evalyn.

"Does she want to die?" asked Elsa.

"I think she wants to stop being afraid," said Evalyn. "Look at me, Erik. She loves you … both of you, and your Papa. Her mind is just … well, sick … and she does not know what she does or says sometimes."

"But she cut herself … with Papa's razor! She wants to die!" said Erik, his voice raised.

"And she does not want us!" added Elsa.

"If she wanted to die, she would have cut an artery. Remember how we are learning about the human anatomy? There is an artery here," she said, pointing to her wrist, "and here," she added, pointing to the triangular soft tissue at the crease of her arm. "Maybe her mind is telling her that if her body hurts, then her mind will not hurt so much. Understand? I am going to try to learn more about this when I return home."

"You will tell others?" asked Erik, eyes wide.

"No, of course not. I would not share this. Please do not worry about that. I think we should not worry your Papa either. He has enough to think about with this storm. He will learn of it when he sees her arm, but you must not make him know that it upsets you. We can speak of it together. Agreed? And, also, we must all pray for your Mama. Can we pray together now?"

******

For about an hour, the three took turns reading aloud from Evalyn's *Aesop's Fables*. The children drank warm milk. When they began yawning, Evalyn, for the first time since her employment, followed them into their bedroom. After whispering another prayer, she brushed her fingers softly across their forehead and bid them a restful night. Fatigued, but too agitated by the evening's events to consider sleep, she sat alone in the dim parlor. Her mind pursued fragments of the past seven months. Storm winds seemed to her to shift and sway the home; shutters knocked exasperatingly. She imagined Lias in the lighthouse or on the shore. She hoped he and others were not in peril.

Agnes slept, oblivious.

A closing door startled Evalyn awake. Disoriented, she righted herself in the wingback chair and turned to see Lias at the threshold. Daylight was just beginning to awaken the home's interior.

"Miss Gray?"

"I … um … could not …" She looked around trying to remember where she was. "The storm … is all well?" Her eyes adjusted to the muted room. Before her stood a man wearied by work and worry.

"The storm abated. It not so terrible. But a schooner … crew of four … they try to make harbor before storm and caught on Morris shore. They are in Station. I give them cot and blanket and coffee. They are safe. One man has wound on arm, but I bandage. I will eat and sleep a little and then return. They repair boat today and make to Charleston soon today, maybe. Or tomorrow."

"Oh, I am thankful! The children and I … Mrs. Larsson …" Evalyn stumbled over her words, attempting to right them. "We have prayed for safety."

"Is all well here?" Lias, though fatigued, questioned her with his tone and countenance.

"Um … yes. Everyone must still be asleep. Can I get you some food?" she asked cheerfully, belying a rising unease.

"No, thank you. I will get. You rest in room. Sky clearing. Perhaps your boat will arrive this morning."

******

When Evalyn descended the stairs a few hours later, bright, clear, late-morning light penetrated the home's interior, and Agnes was setting on the table a bowl of warm hash and a plate of sliced cantaloupe. Despite the warm and humid July morning, she wore a long-sleeved white blouse with her floor-length skirt. The looseness of the sleeve concealed the bandage beneath. Lias, clean shaven and clothed, adjusted suspenders as he entered the room behind Evalyn. Agnes admonished her with a fleeting glance before disappearing into the pantry. Erik and Elsa appeared together, their hair disheveled. Evalyn was pleased to realize expectations regarding dress and punctuality lessened on weekends. They approached their father, who stood to hug them.

"The storm was bad?" asked Erik first. "I tried to not sleep. To wait for you."

"We prayed!" added Elsa.

Lias studied his children. Their faces still revealed a strained flush. "You worry? You have sleeping trouble?"

"A little," answered Elsa, looking at Erik for support.

"A little," added Erik. He glanced at his mother but did not make eye contact with her. She busied herself as they spoke.

"Storm not so bad as sounded. Your prayers keep me safe … and men …" Lias sat back down at the table and shared with them in some English, but mostly Swedish, what he had told Evalyn earlier that morning. "This is strong lighthouse and strong house," he announced as Agnes completed setting the table with a stack of toast. He smiled warmly at her. "All sleep well and safe. That is most important. Let us bless this meal."

Evalyn folded her hands before her and bowed her head. But before Lias completed his expression of thankfulness, she looked up. Erik and Elsa stared at her, wide-eyed, debilitated. Evalyn shook her head slightly, offered her cohorts a smile to assuage apprehension, and bowed her head again, hoping they would follow her lead.

Blessing completed, all those seated in the dining room on Morris Island concentrated on their breakfast.

The skiff captain's knock startled everyone at the table. Agnes gasped and dropped her fork, causing bits of hash to catapult from her plate onto the table. Lias bounded to the door. "Come in. I told Miss Gray that you were smart man to not come in storm."

Evalyn took her last bite of breakfast as to not leave waste, excused herself, and bounded up the stairs to retrieve her valise.

"Breakfast?" asked Lias of the man standing at his threshold.

"No, sar. Thank ya'."

As quickly as Evalyn ascended the stairs, she descended. She tried to squelch the relief she felt at leaving the Larsson home. Imminent was Lias' discovery of the previous night's drama, and she wished not to be present. She hoped Saturday and Sunday would afford an opportunity for at least some quieting before another of Agnes' storms flashed furiously. Plus, she had devised upon waking a plan to learn as much as she could about Agnes' mental condition. Yet, her own voice and that of her friend Samuel's nagged her conscience. *Just teach.* But throughout the early morning hours, she had convinced herself that she might play a larger role in the lives of the Larssons. Perhaps discovering more about the mind's inner workings could be passed onto the children and bring them a grain of understanding and comfort about their mother's illness. Agnes' mind, she suspected, was a fractured organ, not easily or even possibly repaired. But comprehending it, at least somewhat, might be a tonic for a hurting family.

Since her mother and stepfather likely assumed her stay on Morris Island would extend through the weekend, Evalyn appealed to the wagon driver to take her to the ferry platform instead of stopping at her James Island home. She planned to visit the Charleston library at the corner of Church and Broad streets and to inquire of a psychologist. It would cost her a week's wages to pay for the extra mileage in the wagon, the ferry ticket to and from Charleston, a light lunch, and the book or books she would probably not have the fortitude to resist purchasing – as books were her weakness; but, a trip to the city was overdue, would provide distraction, and might broaden her inquisitive teacher's mind.

When she arrived at the ferry, it was still early enough that a handful of weekenders had not yet crossed. Charleston, though in view from the James Island shore on Wappoo Creek, offered culture and indulgences rare to islanders, whose dirty, calloused, and sweaty hands seldom experienced either. Some ferry passengers at times simply desired or needed services not offered on James Island, but which were aplenty in the largish coastal city. Saturday was a fuller day for the ferry captain; routes increased, and occasionally a last, late trip involved revelers who partook too heavily in libations offered at a Charleston tavern or private party.

While crossing, Evalyn inquired of the late afternoon ferry schedule. No rules were posted nor enforced, but Charleston's unspoken etiquette required that single ladies be escorted during and after the supper hour. She needed to finish her business and catch the late afternoon ferry back to James Island.

Evalyn's first stop was the Charleston Library Society, established even before America existed. British men with a homeland yearning began amassing English books covering all subjects, including the sciences, travel, architecture, and literature. Prior to the Civil War, men were the Library's frequent callers, but weary years spent reconstructing the old Southern city loosened reins on societal mores. Women coming and going raised few eyebrows.

Evalyn ensconced herself at a walnut table close to a shelf housing books of psychological tradition, phrenology, and Scottish mental philosophy. The clerk who assisted her explained that psychology was becoming a flourishing profession. Scientific studies on the mind were prevalent at Harvard and Yale, with new findings published frequently, he told her.

"William James is who you want to read," said the clerk, an enthusiastic middle-aged man with a limp. "He convinced Harvard to let him teach their first psychology course some years back, the '70s I believe." He rubbed at his upper thigh while he spoke. Evalyn assumed it was a nagging war wound. Men carried whole bullets, bits of shot, and metal that would have cost them their lives to remove. But the foreign objects nagged and pained their hosts for life.

Immersed in James' essays, Evalyn read over and over again his description of one's "mental state ... aware of itself only from within; it grasps what we call its own content, nothing more." James hinted of his own psychological crisis and that of his father's, of hallucinations, and of frequent bouts of panic. She pulled a journal out of her bag and began to write notes she might abbreviate for the children, or share in full with Lias. James' published discourse on habit seemed promising and constructive: "It alone is what keeps us all within the bounds of ordinance ... it holds the miner in his darkness ...to make the best of a pursuit that disagrees, because there is no other for which we are fitted …"

Habit? Could Agnes control her rampant mind with rigid routine?

Evalyn's spirits lifted, momentarily, until she read a few paragraphs of James' teachings on happiness and free-will: "There are persons whose existence is little more than a series of zigzags, as now one tendency and now another gets the upper hand. Their spirit wars with their flesh, they wish for incompatibles, wayward impulses interrupt their most deliberate plans, and their lives are one long drama of repentance and of effort to repair misdemeanors and mistakes."

Agnes.

An ache rose in her temple. Still, she opened one more book pulled randomly off the Library's shelf. Its title intrigued: *Diseases of the Mind and the Question of Patient Restraints.* The book's damaged, flimsy spine failed to maintain its contents; when Evalyn drew back is hard cover, the pages fluttered open, revealing drawings contributed by members of The American Neurological Association. Evalyn felt the muscles in her neck tense and a discomfort knot her stomach as she read that the organization was founded by Civil War physicians witnessing the effects of brain and other injuries on soldiers' behaviors.

A man, head cocked unnaturally to one side, was bound in a white suit secured with leather wraps and buckles. Another man's face held a grimace; his hands and feet appeared tightly tied to a chair in which he sat.

Evalyn snapped the book closed.

Before leaving the Library, just as St. Michael's chime announced loudly the second hour to everyone in earshot, Evalyn asked to see a directory. In her notebook, she wrote addresses of two psychologists. She needed a bite to eat and drink. The ache in her head worsened.

Adjacent to a bookseller at Market and King streets, a cart offered hot cream fritters made to order. Evalyn had overheard one day in Mac's a James Islanders speaking of the nouveau French pastry charming Charlestonians, but she had not considered there would be an opportunity to try one beyond inserting herself into a grand banquet. One fritter and a small pot of Earl Gray tea required little of her legal tender, just a three-cent liberty head, and she had not realized how hungry she was until she bit into the delicate confection.

Revived, Evalyn entered the book shop and inquired immediately after the works of James, as well as a contemporary, a G.

Stanley Hall, mentioned briefly in one of the Library's volumes. Upon her request, the bookseller's slight tilt of the head made her wonder if he thought *her* mad. He studied her for a moment, and then reached his hand toward a stack of pamphlets lying near his ledger. "Just in, in fact. But not one of *your* gentlemen."

His friendly expression conveyed to Evalyn that he had already dismissed the thought that she might be seeking a book for her own mental malady. "Are you a student of the mind?" he asked, somewhat condescendingly, owing to – she assumed – her sex. He handed her a pamphlet.

Evalyn decided to answer directly. "No. I know … um, know someone who suffers. I thought I might learn well, more … perhaps … to possibly help. What is this?" She reviewed the cover's title, *An Essay on Studies in Hysteria and the Case of Anna O*, by Sigmund Freud.

"A new man who has garnered some attention in this mysterious field of mind study … Freud."

Without acknowledging the bookseller, Evalyn thumbed through the pamphlet, resting on the words "torment … lethargy … phobia."

"Perhaps your suffering soul is an Anna O?" The bookseller's voice grated. *Was it because of his tone or his words?* Evalyn innards again shifted. The cream fritter settled uneasily in her stomach.

"What is the price?"

For the pamphlet, Evalyn would have to forfeit her nickel. She hoped the writings of Freud would help in some way. Before paying the bookseller, however, she asked to see the teaching category. Walking toward the shelves, she preached inwardly a momentary sermon on self-control, but Appleton's latest *American Standard Geographies* seized her. She owned an outdated, limited volume. The one she held, she noted while gingerly turning a few pages, included more detailed maps and illustrations of people groups, wildlife, architecture, and native plants. The book would allow her to weave a wider web of understanding and perspective of the large world – one she knew not personally but envisaged all the same. *A curious student teaches curious students.* Pulling herself away from the schoolbooks' section, she was enticed by a side glance to peruse a title lying on its side atop a low shelf.

"Oh, I haven't put that one away yet," said the bookseller. "just unpacked it."

"I'll take it as well," said Evalyn, spontaneously. Without investigating its contents or noting the cost, Evalyn resolved *Chesterfield's Art of Letter Writing Simplified* was exactly what the Larsson family needed to improve and reinforce their English. No matter if they had no one in their lives with whom to correspond in English. They would become proficient at penning letters to imaginary individuals, if necessary, until that formal, important skill flowed naturally.

Each bound schoolbook cost 10 cents.

"The time, please sir."

"It is exactly 3:00," he responded, finishing a neat tuck of the brown paper with which he wrapped each book.

"Thank you." Evalyn slid the volumes into her bag and hurried to find one of the two psychologist's offices before making her way to the ferry landing. Her remaining time allowed for a quick visit to only one. She chose the office at the corner of Broad and Rutledge, situated en route to the landing. Evalyn walked apprehensively on the brick sidewalk, fashioned by the formerly enslaved. Horses clopped along the narrow street pulling wagons of various dimensions and styles. The tea hour just ending, few pedestrians crowded the late summer streets.

Despite independence from their British mother country 100 years earlier, old habits refused a complete snuffing out; comfortable Charlestonians still took tea and enjoyed afternoon cakes and biscuits. A priest acknowledged her with a slight nod; two men in suits and bowlers did not. She wondered whether the psychologist took tea. She looked again at her note to read the name and number, a Franklin Wundt, 351 Broad Street. And would he see her, even for a moment? *Was seeking a psychologist's advice crossing a line?*

Evalyn drew in the procession of two- and three-storied gabled homes, all with doors entering not the homes, as was the case with simple clapboard houses on James Island, but far-reaching columned piazzas. She realized suddenly that although she was familiar with the exterior distinctness of Charleston's homes, an opportunity to enter one had not been available to her. With trepidation, she wondered how she might knock. *Was there entering etiquette?*

She stopped in front of a house that matched almost perfectly those flanking either side. Muted taupe-painted stucco over brick contrasted with black hurricane shutters. Number 351 was painted on a plaque above the name Wundt, Applied Psychology. Fortunately, a heavy iron door knocker adorned with a small forged pineapple motif was attached to the outer piazza door. She knocked timidly at first. Before she could try a more forceful knock, a slight, young black girl appeared. Evalyn supposed her age to be the same as Erik's.

"Yes, ma'am? You has an appointment with Mr. Wundt?"

"Uh, no … I only wish to speak to him for a moment. I live on James Island and cannot …"

"This way, ma'am." With lively steps, the bonneted girl led Evalyn into a small parlor just off the lower piazza. "He finishin' with someone. You waits here. I gots to go help Mama get his supper ready. He'll be along soon."

"Thank you so much."

The girl flashed a cheerful smile before disappearing through a doorway. Evalyn relieved a detained breath. She heard two men speaking in whispers. A different door than the one she had entered closed, and then footsteps approached. She stood up.

"Oh. I was not aware I had yet another patient."

"I … no. Mr. Wundt?"

"Yes, of course. And you are?"

The man before Evalyn was short, stout, and sported a perfectly symmetrical handlebar moustache.

"Evalyn Gray. I am sorry, Mr. Wundt. I do not have an appointment. I live on James Island and I teach, and I really must catch a returning ferry soon, but I have to ask your advice, as a psychologist. It's for someone I know." Words spilled, pell-mell. "She, or should I say the one for whom I am inquiring, but yes, a lady ... I have gathered information at the library ... a book, Freud, from the bookseller's ..."

"Miss, please sit," instructed Mr. Wundt, his tone hinting at exasperation. "*Why* have you come?"

Evalyn grabbed her thoughts and aligned them. "So sorry, sir. I have come because I would like to ask you what help is available ... possible ... for someone who suffers in the mind?"

"Her symptoms?"

"Well, I believe she is paranoid and most certainly anxious," shared Evalyn, "and she is easily agitated."

"Ah ..." Mr. Wundt pulled himself inward and rested an elbow in one hand, the thumb just supporting his lower lip.

"She believes animals are watching her."

"Hmmm ... I see." He nodded, waiting for her to reveal more.

Evalyn hesitated. She wanted to describe Easter Sunday. Instead she blurted: "She has cut herself of late ... with a razor blade."

She had his attention.

Mr. Wundt furrowed his brow. His gaze, previously unfocused on anything in particular, fixated directly at her. His lids widened, exposing more pupil than Evalyn cared to see. His stare immediately unnerved her.

"But she did *not* try to take her life … only light cuts. She feels a dark weight, a …"

"I must see her. Cutting is a serious consequence of hysteria. There are some methods … medications. Institutions, if her issues are …"

"No!" Evalyn stood. And though she realized her discourteous tone, she continued. "Pardon me, sir. But your suggestions are impossible. She cannot come …"

"Then why do you trouble me today with your visit?" He feigned no courteousness.

"I just thought, perhaps, you might offer advice … some techniques, on how we, her family, might help her … I cannot pay much, but …"

"You clearly do not comprehend psychology, Miss. The mind … it is, well, complicated. There is no quick fix. If this person you speak of cannot be seen by a specialist," his voice wavered and then rose, "and if this family of hers will not institutionalize her to learn what help might be available, then my only advice is this …"

Evalyn took a step back as he leaned in, measuring his words while he glared. "… be on guard and aware and know that someone may need to restrain her because she will likely harm herself or ultimately harm others. I have seen this in other patients. If someone is to the point of self-harming, the harming continues and becomes more intense and dangerous. Prepare for *that*, Miss Gray."

The clock's piercing "ting, ting" broke the tense exchange.

"I must go. I am sorry to have troubled you, Mr. Wundt. Good day."

"Good day, Miss," his demeanor softened as Evalyn stepped onto the sidewalk. "I hope, for your sake and the lady of whom you speak – and anyone else with whom she is in contact – that a specialist's help is reconsidered. You may send word if you wish to make an appointment."

Evalyn acknowledged his words with a polite nod and stepped onto Broad Street. Hastily, while still maintaining decorum, she walked to the ferry landing at the street's end. Her heart's beating pummeled the inside of her chest cavity, a blacksmith's hammer against anvil.

The ferry master, a tanned young man with hair bleached by prolonged sun exposure, huffed irritation while unlatching the rope he had already hung to signal he was ready to set ferry to course.

"I apologize," offered Evalyn, stepping onto the wooden surface. "Thank you." She handed him a few of her remaining coins and steadied herself for the trip across the Ashley River and directly into Wappoo Creek.

Evalyn held onto the railing of the flat-bottom scow, breathed deeply several times to slow the disturbance in her countenance, and contemplated the psychologist's alarming counsel.

THE SHIFT

Evalyn opened her eyes the next morning and noticed immediately the deafening drone of cicadas amassed among trees. Whether on James or Morris Island, she had in summer always awoken to an orchestra of pleasant sounds: the throaty ting of golden- or black-winged warblers or the rhythmic cheeps and caws of glossy blueish-black male grackles and their always mimicking brownish female partners. But the large bugs saved their ominous buzzing for hot summer afternoons. They never buzzed at break of day, at least not in Evalyn's recollection. She propped herself up on her elbows and strained to hear common bird songs and calls. None. The only sound penetrating the dawn was that of the cicadas' rising cacophony.

Evalyn dressed; an unexplainable dread rested upon her.

She found her mother and stepfather on the front porch discussing the cicadas.

"Not a good sign," said her stepfather.

"Not a good sign of what?" asked Evalyn.

"Just not a good sign. Them bugs don't make noise in the early mornin'. Not since I've been on this earth. Not even before a storm, or nothin'."

"It's a cursing sound," added her mother. "And they seem to be getting louder."

They had barely acknowledged Evalyn when she arrived from Charleston the previous evening. They conveyed no concern of her whereabouts or relief that she was not harmed by Friday's storm.

"Goin' to church?" her stepfather asked.

"Yes."

"Ask around."

Evalyn consumed a piece of buttered toast with jam and a cup of black tea before dressing for church. From the notes in her father's bible, the only book of his left to her, she assumed him to be faithful in his attendance. Her mother refused to answer any questions on the matter. And Evalyn had stopped asking her mother to accompany her on Sundays. Since marrying her stepfather, her mother determined less of a need — since he was not particularly faithful. The couple had fallen into holiday regularity, when many other souls like themselves were motivated to put in an appearance.

Evalyn walked into the church yard to find several congregants gathered, heads tilted, perusing a dense stand of pines. As she walked past, she snatched a bit of their conversation: "… makes no sense … the end? … maybe he will address it …"

Already the still, moist late July air sweltered attendees packing pews. Paper fans stirred thick oven air. The group she passed in the yard meandered in and joined others. The hum of anxious voices rose in an effort to be heard over the cicadas.

Evalyn looked around. More attended than usual.

Though Charleston churches were mostly empty during summer months, since congregants of means left for family mountain homes in cooler Flat Rock and Highlands, James Island's churches kept regular attendance. Yet even the pastor seemed surprised when he approached the pulpit and scanned the church's interior.

Murmurings diminished.

"Good morning," he said, louder than usual. "'Search me, God, and know my heart; test me and know my anxious thoughts. See if there is any offensive way in me, and lead me in the way everlasting.' Let us pray for our time in His word in Psalm 139."

"What about them bugs?" called someone behind Evalyn.

"Yeah!" echoed another.

"Let us pray," repeated the pastor, ignoring the extraordinary outbursts; he launched too loudly into: "Lord, we lean not into our own understanding but trust you to show us this morning, every second, minute, and hour, your mysteries, your purposes. Let us all open ourselves to be searched ... to be mindful of our sins of distrust and worry ..." He paused, and more than a few heads lifted and eyes opened, their thoughts wondering if they had missed the "amen."

"... and to know, no matter the trials, *you* will lead us in the way everlasting. Amen. For those of you who brought along your bibles, turn with me now to Psalm ..."

"But preacher ... your thoughts ... the cicadas and their infernal buzzin' this mornin'!" raised an older man on the front row. "We want ta hear what you ..."

"Please ..." interrupted the pastor, his tone straining toward control. "Let us finish this service and then we will address the bugs through our conversation and prayers."

"But ..." tried another.

"*Please* ..."

The flock acquiesced, settling in for the 20-minute recitation, which would be followed by a succession of memorized hymns. After the completion of a final prayer, which again included appeals of trust and understanding of things unseen and unknown, the front row gentleman spoke again, "Before we go, can we …"

"Yes. Let us discuss this phenomenon … this strange occurrence," resumed the pastor.

"I'm gettin' no more eggs from my layers since mid last week," blurted Mrs. Blakenship.

"Mine have diminished, now that I'm thinkin' on it," added one of her contemporaries.

"I watched my bees yesterday just up and leave their hive and fly around in circles like they were in a twister. Kept landin' and swirlin', all confused like, before they just vacated my property," offered one farmer. "Been doin' bees for years and none acted that much a fool."

"A fox upsettin' my dog at all hours last night, even after I lit a lantern and shood 'em. Makin' that accursed screaming sound like the demons knockin' in its head," said a man just five years older than Evalyn; his family was known as established shrimpers, supplying some of the banquet halls and cafes in Charleston. "And I'm not catchin' worth anythin'."

"And now these infernal bugs! What's happenin'?" asked the shrimper's wife. "None like this was goin' on last year before the great cyclone hit and threatened to wipe us out! None like this in my lifetime, that I recall."

Congregants nodded in agreement.

"Negroes is worried, too," inserted another farmer. "Heard ol' Harriet Forest prayin' loud in their field on the way here this mornin'. Ain't none of us can afford to have our late crops, the greens and cabbages, drowned out like last year."

Before the pastor spoke, he pointed to Thomas, who sat at the opposite end of the row on which Evalyn remained seated, hemmed in by others too spellbound to move. Thomas, whose wife perched straight and dutiful, had his hand raised. He stood, and after the pastor's pointing finger gave permission, spoke politely: "Perhaps there are things happening with the sun and the gravitational pull? Perhaps a bad storm is out there in the Atlantic somewhere making the creatures nervous? I think, as the pastor has assured us this morning …"

Thomas looked around, making eye contact with people he had known all his life; his eyes skipped over those of Evalyn's. "… we need not panic, but realize that not all is *known* to us. We take precautions, in case it is a storm, but trust our Lord and pray for his guidance and protection."

Thomas, though young, procured the respect of James Islanders, partly because of his family's long-standing fine character but mainly due to their mercantile, the Island's foremost business for buying and selling. And the MacDonalds were always decent, offering credit and fair terms when times were lean. His words, barely heard over the din rising still steadily from the tall trees beyond the church grounds, appeased. Congregants looked around. Some shrugged and nodded. A few stirred and stood and then others followed. Slowly, they filed out.

"Go in peace and good will," the pastor boomed wearily.

******

"It's the end for certain," declared Evalyn's stepfather. Even though Mac's did not open on Sundays, men often spent Lord's day afternoons in the store's yard discussing the weather, politics, newcomers, crops – bugs. Having conversed with the group, Evalyn's stepfather returned home to share their consensus with Evalyn and her mother.

"Everyone's got their own mind 'bout what's happenin', but many don't have good feelins' about them bugs," he said.

"Thomas reminded us this morning that it could be a hurricane brewing, or some sort of gravitational pull," said Evalyn, while assisting her mother with a few hems before packing for the week.

"Thomas!?" Her mother looked up from a skirt lying across her lap; her needle suspended at her waist. "So, he's the authority?"

Evalyn watched as her stepfather nodded in agreement with his wife; his eyes rolled exaggeratedly.

"It was a suggestion … a reminder for us not to rush to alarm," said Evalyn.

"Well, I guess *his* Mrs. MacDonald can take comfort in having a *husband* who is so resolute."

Evalyn remained silent, bracing against antagonism's bait. She added the last stitch and tied off the thread, cutting it with her front teeth. "I must pack."

"Hmpf!" Her mother's gaze followed Evalyn as she stood up, neatly folded the skirt, and turned to exit the small room. "Back to insanity island then? And leave us to handle this plague alone?"

Her mother's last spiteful thrust tempted Evalyn to react. She took a deep breath and remembered the pastor's last word: peace. While she packed, she resurrected snippets of a hymn she had long forgotten, *Peace Like a River*. Internally she sang the words, partly to cover the loud discord of buzzing insects bothering her nerves, but also to calm resentment for a mother unwilling to unconditionally love and support her.

Evalyn heard her mother announce to her stepfather that she would pay a visit to her friend, Lily Latham. Before she exited the home, she spoke loudly: "I will learn if the ladies of this island have any better explanation, other than *hurricanes or gravity*, causing the merciless noise of these wretched insects!"

Evalyn sighed.

Though packing was rote, after seven months of going and coming, she focused attention on each clothing item's fold, the placing of the pamphlet and books purchased in Charleston, the wrapping of toiletries in a small, hand-sewn, ribbon-adorned bag. She read over the week's lesson plans. She still had another hour to wait. She yearned to be away from the oppression of a house that felt nothing like a home. Yet, discomfort awaited her off James Island as well. *Was there truly anything useful to share with Mr. Larsson?* she questioned. *Might some of the information help Agnes in some small way?*

Despite the piercing outdoor noise, and the clattering inside her head, Evalyn heard the slight click of her door's metal latch, the slow strain of a rusty hinge. Her stepfather peered at her from the door frame. In seven months, she had not suffered his ardor; she assumed her standing as lighthouse teacher had somehow quelled harbored desires. But the man at her threshold leached intentions through his wanton stare.

He pushed open the door further.

"If the world as we know it is ending ..."

"It's not." She backed behind the valise stand to put something between her and her stepfather.

"These bugs! They ain't causin' pain, so why are we worryin'? It's just sound, nothin' more. Why does it bother us so?" He looked out her small window and then back at her, taking a step closer.

"I'm not worrying. What do you want?"

"You think teachin' instead of sewin' makes you better 'n your poor mother? You think …" He moved closer still. "… any man's goin' to *want* you? Thomas didn't."

Evalyn pulled a knitting needle from a yarn ball lying in a basket atop her dresser. "You will not step one foot closer to me! Leave my room!" she yelled, startling his rapt obsession.

"Hush!" He looked back at the door. "I only come in here to see if you need some help packin' for your week on the island."

"You have not asked me once in these seven months if I need help! I know what you came in here for! I will shamelessly share of your lechery with every islander within miles if ever you have a mind to enter my room again or even consider placing one of your repulsive fingers on my person! I have nothing to lose by making your intentions public! Leave!"

"I have no idea what you speak of, girl. You're as batty as that missus you work for. Besides, no one'd ever believe …"

She stepped from behind the stand, pushing the needle toward him. "Leave!"

With a sordid stare embalmed on his face, he slithered backwards through the open door.

Evalyn rammed the needle back into the yarn ball, checked the room for any unpacked items, and snapped close the valise. She left the room and walked purposefully past her stepfather, who stood vacant on the front porch.

"Where are you … your wagon is not … Evalyn!"

Even though her legs wobbled, she showed him no acknowledgement. She exited the yard gate and marched down the dirt road in the direction of water, and a light, and madness. She cared nothing for islanders who might notice her walking, instead of riding in a wagon, toward her weekly employment. But then the tears came, reminding her of propriety. She allowed just a few to glide down her cheeks. No houses occupied a stretch of several yards, so she stopped, dropped her valise at her side, and pulled a small handkerchief from her apron pocket. She had indulged herself with seven, one for every day of the week, each hand-made and adorned with delicate stitches that formed an E.G. at one corner. She sniffled into the cloth and wiped under her lids, dotting the corner of both eyes. She looked at the pine trees lined up all the way to where the marsh began. *Quiet.* She realized the vibrating clamor had ceased. She strained to hear the sound, even a faint tapering off. Nothing. *Quiet.* No bugs, no bird song;

nothing. She felt a rumbling under her feet. Assuming her driver was catching up to her, Evalyn wiped once more under her nose, stuffed the handkerchief into her pocket, and picked up her valise. But when she turned to look back up the road, no one approached. And the ground shook no more.

******

Evalyn sat drenched and defeated in the scorching skiff. Her regular driver had not turned up to rescue her on the road; she imagined her spiteful stepfather conveying to him an untruth when he arrived to pick her up as usual. A negro man driving a small cart and mule offered her respite for the last quarter mile. He had sung low and steady *Amazing Grace*, interjecting commands to the mule. He asked no questions, except where she needed dropping off. He had asked for no coin, but she insisted he take one.

A straw hat did little to shield Evalyn from the baking heat. Normally the weekly boat ride to Morris enlivened. But the hot, dead air agitated further her awareness of what might transpire when she arrived. She tried concentrating on the upcoming week's lessons, of her duties as teacher, not as meddler in the private affairs of her employers.

The boat's bow cut the still water. The skiff captain hummed.

Amazing Grace. Evalyn glanced up at him and then toward the

lighthouse, which grew with each row.

She was thankful to be away from her stepfather but tensed at

the thought of facing him at week's end. As much as she tried to focus

wholly on teaching, even opening her bag and paging through

Chesterfield's Art of Letter Writing Simplified to figure out how the lessons

might factor into daily studies, Evalyn's mind drifted unintentionally.

She imagined various scenarios that might help Agnes: Calming habits.

Charts and checklists. Writing letters to herself … to her demons.

Was a specialist's attention the only real solution?

The skiff captain's back to her, Evalyn returned to her bag the

Chesterfield's Art of Letter Writing Simplified and pulled out *An Essay on*

Studies in Hysteria and the Case of Anna O. The young doctor's writings

described hysteria as fear and anxiety. Unrealistic, irrational fear, but

fear that takes one beyond the bounds of decorum. Hysterical thoughts

cause one to become uninhibited. There is the natural fight or flight

instinct, but a person suffering phobias and paranoia exaggerates those

tendencies. Some trepidation and delusion are brought on by trauma or

tragedy. Evalyn learned that Anna O, a pseudonym so as to protect the family of which the young woman belonged, suffered intermittent somnambulism, involuntary eye movements, hydrophobia, unexplained paralysis, and language confusion – all brought on by the deaths of her sister and father from tuberculosis.

Evalyn, engrossed in the pamphlet, startled when the skiff captain spoke. "Nearly there, Miss."

When she looked up, the dock was within view. On the dock stood Lias, rigid, a frown heavy on his face.

Evalyn looked beyond Lias for signs of the children, his wife. She stuffed the pamphlet back into her bag and readied herself. Lias waited, a slight stoop to his broad shoulders and his fists clenched tight at his side.

"You were not supposed to come," he said, as the bow drew closer to the dock. "I sent word ... a fisherman ..."

"What? No ... I received no word. Why?"

"Take her back." He leaned over the boat and opened a fist to reveal a few coins. "Please forgive," he said, making eye contact with both Evalyn and the skiff captain. And then he repeated, "Take her back" to the skiff captain, who accepted tentatively the offered fare from Lias' opened palm.

Lias turned and took a few steps toward the lighthouse.

"No!" Evalyn put her valise onto the dock. She extended her hand. "I am not going back. Please, help me to the dock."

One long stride took Lias back to the dock's edge. He crouched down. "You must not," he implored, ignoring the skiff captain, who was tying a cleat hitch to the dock pile so the boat would not move. "Difficulties," he whispered, leaning in closer to her. "Too many difficulties." His face seeped sadness.

"I cannot return," she said. "Not today. Difficulties at home for me as well." She extended her hand again. "I have information. I learned much that may help. Please."

"Nothing will …"

"*Please*, Mr. Larsson." She extended her hand rigidly, determined. "Whatever is happening here, as you said before, it is better for me to be here, especially for the children, than to not be here."

Expressing a defeated sigh, Lias grasped her slight hand with his sturdy one.

"Sir …" the skiff captain opened his dark hand to offer back the coins.

"You keep," said Lias, picking up Evalyn's bag. "Safe return."

They walked, measured and silently, for only a few seconds before he spoke. "She does not want you here. I must lie and tell her boat could not take you back. She is sleeping now. I give her whiskey in her tea. But she will wake, and her mind will not stop. The insects, early today. They frighten ... They make her mind believe they are demons to harm her. And the crabs ... those small crabs, they are ..."

"Fiddler crabs?"

"Yes. Fiddler. She believes they are spiders. My wife ... she believes these fiddler crabs will get into our home and eat her body. She said the earth moves and cracks and pushes them to her ..." As he revealed the weekend drama, his arm raised and his large palm flexed and extended forward to illustrate his words. "Me ... the children ... she frightens when she speaks of such things."

He stopped speaking for a few paces.

At the back door of the home, on the boardwalk that connected the home to the lighthouse, Lias' hulk released a sob. He dropped her bag beside him, bowed his head into his large hands, and held his breath.

"Oh, sir …" Evalyn yearned to disperse his agony with a healing touch. She reached up to stroke his hands just as he pulled them away from his face.

"I am sorry … so sorry." His face contorted as he struggled to keep tears at bay.

"No … please do not be sorry. I cannot imagine your bewilderment … your worry." For the second time as a paid teacher, she touched her employer. Her hand rested on his, which were clasped prayer-like in front of him.

******

The next morning, while splashing water on her face, a still-statue crane fly perched at the rim of the porcelain basin. Instead of reflexively smashing it, Evalyn dabbed her face with a towel and studied it. Its straight, slender, rigid body was balanced symmetrically by two narrow, transparent wings. Not one of its six pylon-like legs twitched or trembled. Evalyn had only ever seen such a bug fly confused and careless, not remain motionless, seemingly meditative. Its stillness is what caught her attention.

She finished her toilette, eyeing the crane fly once more before moving to the other side of her room where her day dress waited, draped over a chair. She dressed, dreamlike, reflecting on the prior evening.

Lias had admitted to Evalyn that he had also mixed a bit of laudanum, left over from Agnes' breakdown in Sweden, into her tea and whiskey concoction. He said he was desperate to subdue her nervous, fearful state, which was troubling to the children. She drank the tonic without complaint and had eventually succumbed to exhaustion. She rested deeply. Her semi-unconscious state had allowed Lias, after he composed himself, to gather the children at the interior base of the lighthouse so that Evalyn could share what she learned in Charleston.

Though early evening, the late-August South Carolina heat had pressed in on Evalyn as she tried to speak plainly. Lias held a small candle; the children's faces were eager for her words, but Evalyn wilted as much from their concerned demeanor as from the oven-like temperature pent up in the small space. She gave them a summary of her studies in the library and what she had read so far in the pamphlet, but mostly she shared James' ideas on how establishing rigid daily habits provided comfortable boundaries for some people struggling with … She paused, grappling with the right words to describe Agnes so as not to heap more unease on the already overwhelmed family. Evalyn finally settled on "malady of the mind." She remembered reading the phrase several times. It seemed less vivid than "hysteria."

"She is sick. I have said this ... know this," said Erik.

"But can she heal?" implored Elsa.

"I do not know ..." said Evalyn, suddenly wishing she had listened to Samuel. *Be a teacher only.* She was teaching, sharing, what she had learned. But the subject was not familiar to her and not one she had been hired to teach. She was learning right along with them. *I have no business ...* She reached out to touch the cool wall.

"Miss Gray, are you well?" Lias grabbed her elbow to steady her.

"Yes. Just felt faint for a moment. I am fine."

"The heat. And all this ... I am sorry for you to be a part of this ..."

"I am fine," repeated Evalyn, adding, "I must ask you, because of what I read, did she ever suffer a trauma? One of the reasons for a malady of the mind is because of trauma. But sometimes there is no reason at all."

"I know of no trauma. Only good parents, good life on her family farm … and then we marry."

Evalyn could not see clearly his face, but grief penetrated his tone.

Lias looked at his children. They needed to see resolve, not despair. "I think we try what you say you learn from your reading, Miss Gray," he said, with effort. "We can try to keep all the same for her, calm and the same, and we will pray that she will be helped. You agree, children?"

They nodded their heads. Elsa let out breath as if she were holding onto it until he spoke.

"So, we do not question your Mama or ask her to do a thing that is not part of her daily tasks. We must be different with her than we are with each other. We do not have ex … ex …"

"Ex-pec-tations," finished Erik.

Evalyn could not help herself from smiling at him – for knowing the difficult English word.

"Yes. Expectations," reiterated Lias. He put his large hand affectionately on his son's head. "We do not react when she sees something, hears something, feels something that is not real. We speak calm and nice to her, always."

"But Papa ..." whimpered Elsa.

Lias cupped his daughter's chin with his other hand and tilted her face to him. He continued: "And if she does a thing that makes you afraid, you leave and come to me. The lighthouse will be safe place. Yes? When I receive payment next month, I will call for this person ... this Mr. Wundt, who Miss Gray has spoken to. He may have more help ... medicines, for your poor Mama. You know, children, she is ill – not evil. Yes? We must not give up on her. We must help her as we can."

Elsa broke. She stepped into Lias' sturdy midsection and buried her face. Lias stroked her blond hair and leaned down to kiss the top of her head as she cried.

With his father and sister distracted, Erik stepped toward Evalyn and grasped tightly her hand. His dread grip on her caused an ache in her chest.

When Lias dried Elsa's eyes with his shirt sleeve, Erik released the secure hold on his teacher.

Before opening the lighthouse door and dismissing the reticent party, Lias had prayed for his wife and the mother of his children. He had forced a broad smile, wished them a "good night," and pulled the heavy metal door toward him. The children maneuvered the boardwalk while Evalyn had paused and looked back to see the faint glow of Lias' lantern pass the small windows as he ascended to the lighthouse tower.

That rising glow, and the way the children had lingered at their bedroom doorway, as if alluded sleep could postpone an uncertain future, seeped into a crevice of her consciousness. Long after that night, Evalyn could recall the exact softness of the illumination as it passed the lighthouse window — could visualize the stoop in Elsa's shoulders and the way Erik held the door handle before wishing her a good night. Long after, she had wondered why *those* particular moments. Before the shattering.

Evalyn tried to clear her mind of the previous evening before she descended the familiar stairway the next morning. With every step on the creaky wooden stairs, she contemplated both what she would teach and how she would "be" with Agnes.

"Good morning," Evalyn said. As soon as she entered the dining room and saw Agnes, she was surprised to see that Agnes appeared refreshed. No frenzied glint showed in her eyes. No residual heaviness from the laudanum and whiskey showed on her face or in her movements.

"Yes. Good morning," answered Agnes.

The children, already seated at the table, feigned smiles.

Lias launched into the stratagem conceived the previous night. "Miss Gray has purchased new book," he directed toward his wife. "We can all learn. We write letters ... to anyone, and no one ..."

"In English, Mama," said Elsa.

"I will help translate for you," added Erik.

"We can pretend to write to someone or something," explained Evalyn.

"Pre ... tend?" inquired Agnes.

Lias answered her in Swedish. She nodded her head and repeated, "Pretend ... yes."

"The book explains how letter writing is an excellent ... good ... way to improve English skills," said Evalyn.

"Also, to prepare for hurricane time, we will all have lists of duties. Yes?" said Lias.

Agnes nodded in agreement.

Lying beside Lias' plate were four small pieces of paper. He handed a piece to each person at the table. "You may already do these things, but this will help you to know all that needs to be completed and it will help me to know all *will* be completed."

Agnes took her piece of paper, studied it, placed it beside her plate, and then concentrated on her breakfast. Lias glanced quickly at his children, winked, and followed it with a reassuring smile.

"Does anyone have questions about their duties?"

"No, Papa," the children answered in unison.

Agnes paused from eating; she spoke to Lias in Swedish. Evalyn ascertained by their tone that she was simply asking questions regarding the list. Calm and agreeable. Evalyn drew a satisfied breath.

After dishes were cleared, Evalyn set on the dining table *Chesterfield's Art of Letter Writing Simplified,* along with several sheets of paper. "If you fold the paper, like so, it becomes like a book, if you would like to write to your journal as if it is a fictitious ... not real, person. Write what is happening in your world, on this island, in your home. Write things you learn. Write your feelings ... your fears."

Erik translated some of the words for his mother.

Evalyn tried not to look at Agnes, who stood at the end of the table, straight backed, rigid, and still as the crane fly perched earlier on her porcelain basin. In Agnes' hand was her list, which Evalyn assumed included "write" as a mandate. When Evalyn handed her a piece of paper, Agnes pulled the dining chair away from the table and sat down. Then Evalyn opened Chesterfield's book and began to read slowly the first lesson. When Agnes looked at one of her children and interrupted in Swedish, Elsa or Erik extended an explanation and, upon seeing her satisfied, nodded to Evalyn to continue.

"You may now write," said Evalyn, after the book's first instructions were communicated.

Agnes stared at her paper and then past the dining table to the window. Evalyn tried not to linger on her, making herself available to the children instead. Agnes sat, mesmerized, for several minutes. From their bent states, Elsa and Erik glanced at one another but continued writing. The only sound in the room was of pencils scratching against paper. Elsa finally spoke, "Mama, do you need help?" Agnes did not answer. She seemed lost in the clear glass panes and expanse of sea and sky beyond. "Mama." Without answering her daughter, she picked up a pencil and began to write. She seemed to calculate each letter's formation and read and reread each punctuated sentence.

Evalyn longed to know the content on Agnes' paper, but she dared not question her. The fact that she was actually writing gave Evalyn hope that the task somehow proved therapeutic to Agnes' afflicted psyche.

"You spell light, l-i-t-e?" she asked her children.

They both thought a moment; Elsa wrote it on her slate. "It is l-i-g-h-t, correct Miss Gray?"

"Yes."

"See, Mama." She showed Agnes her slate. "The 'g' and 'h' are silent. You do not hear them."

Erik got up from his seat, walked to the end of the table, and pulled out a dictionary from the middle of a stack of books. "Here, Mama." He smiled at her. "This makes it easier."

"Thank you," she said, before bowing her head to her paper.

After about 15 minutes of writing, Agnes stood, pushed her chair back, and exited the home. The children froze. As quickly as she left, she returned. She wiped the edge of her mouth with her sleeve and sat back down. "I am sorry," she said, looking around the table. "Paper move … letters move … I feel, sick." She put her hands to her pale cheeks.

Evalyn saw Erik open his mouth to speak, but he looked at her first and she shook her head faintly. He understood and went back to writing.

"I hope you feel better, Mama. I feel nauseous, too, sometimes," said Elsa.

"Nauseous … is word for sick stomach?"

"Yes, Mama."

Agnes smiled at Elsa and then resumed writing.

Evalyn waited all week for other signs, for Agnes' eyes to empty of light – for hard lines of tension to strain her face. For some shift in the unusually composed demeanor, or a murmuring from Lias or the children about an imagined sound or sighting. Everyone held their breath throughout the week and waited. Yet, the "moving paper incident" happened only once, and Evalyn considered that maybe Agnes simply needed spectacles for reading.

With dutiful, soldier-like consistency, Agnes carried with her the list, busied herself with chores and letter writing, and appeared no more prone to lunacy than Evalyn or anyone else in the Larsson family.

On Friday afternoon when Lias happened upon Evalyn in the stairwell, while Agnes was collecting eggs from the henhouse, Evalyn almost blurted her desire to know the letters' contents. But she tempered her curiosity and instead said to him, "She seems well this week."

"So well," said Lias. "I am so grateful for suggestions. I pray she will stay well. Thank you." He walked past her a few steps and then turned, "Her letters ... they are tied with string and I believe she keeps them in box under bed. I do not know contents, but I believe she writes about ... lighthouse. She asked this week many questions about lighthouse." He paused, and then looked out the window toward the chicken coop. His voice lowered. "She asked if light from lighthouse takes away dark. What do you think ...''? A door opened. He turned abruptly. "Thank you, Miss Gray."

Agnes entered the home with a basket of eggs, and Evalyn continued up the stairs to her room to pack.

Later that day, Evalyn left the island on the boat that would take her to expected tension awaiting her at her home on James Island; but she already had a plan: to lock herself away in her room "to prepare for lessons," except when her mother was home.

THE EARTHQUAKE

Evalyn awoke the next Tuesday morning able to apply a new vocabulary word she had taught the children the day before: *petrichor*. She had broken the word down to its Latin and Greek cores; *petro* meant rock or stone and *ichor* referenced fluid or watery substance. She leaned her face close to her bedroom's opened window and breathed in the rain-soaked earth. Petrichor was the pleasant smell accompanying rain after a period of warm or hot dry weather, she reiterated to Erik and Elsa during further lessons. She knew the word had been a more difficult one to introduce to the children. She planned to have them walk outside for a moment so they could also experience petrichor's tangibility.

August had been particularly hot on the sea islands. Hot, humid, and almost unbearable. Any rain, no matter how brief, was a relief. Although the heat stifled indoors, outdoors was worse. Thus, their jaunts along the shoreline lessened. Evalyn looked forward to lower temperatures in September and hoped August's end meant summer's end as well.

The prior weekend had been uneventful for Evalyn. Her stepfather had avoided her, and her him. She hoped her warning to him the previous Sunday resounded in his consciousness to such a degree that he would never again approach her wantonly.

Lias told Evalyn during a quick and private moment in the stairwell that Agnes, for the most part, sailed quietly through the weekend. Saturday evening she awoke to a "disturbance on the roof" and "noises in the cellar." He had appeased her by checking both, and then held her until she returned to sleep.

Evalyn blushed when she envisioned the intimate scene – Agnes' hair splayed across her husband's broad shoulders. The discomfiture ceased as quickly as it came upon her, however, as she recalled a news article in Sunday morning's newspaper. Evalyn paled as Lias spoke. A couple in Summerville expressed the exact same. A "disturbance" outside the home. She was certain the report also mentioned both the roof and the cellar. But nothing was amiss when the husband checked. *An odd coincidence?* Evalyn vowed to re-read the article when she returned to James Island.

Lias expressed that he had expected the brief and partial solar eclipse during the Sunday past to alarm Agnes; while at work in the lighthouse perch, he had noted the gradual darkening and rushed to distract her until it passed. She had not noticed, or she did not mention it if she had. He said she spent much of the weekend writing, when not busy with other duties on her list.

All in all, though, Lias confided that he was relieved – that maybe his wife's mental ailment was not as severe as he had thought. Before, in Sweden, her mania had gradually increased with no respite. Perhaps she was mending. His optimistic expressions were catching. Evalyn noticed lifted spirits in the children as well.

Evalyn brought more paper with her for the new school week, and the letter writing continued. The new geography book agreed with Agnes as well. Several times during their lessons, she wandered into the dining room to look at a map, point to Sweden, and make inquiries to the children in Swedish about other places studied. *She misses her homeland*, thought Evalyn.

Lias prepared for a visiting lighthouse-keeper-in-training. Mr. Bennett had written to inform of the young apprentice, who would stay to shadow Lias for only a few days before moving over to Sullivan's Island. Lias told his family he planned to bunk the visitor in the Life Saving Station. Even though there was a small extra bedroom off the pantry, Evalyn thought it wise of Lias to keep the guest away from the house – just in case.

Tuesday's rain left the day still and humid, much like most August days, and the children asked during breakfast if they could fish for flounder and then take a swim in the ocean, after the morning's schoolwork and after chores. Granted permission, they perspired cheerfully inside the home until all was completed.

Elsa had one bathing outfit, the standard black, knee-length, puffed-sleeve wool dress. Although women and girls in Charleston might sport a bathing outfit adorned with a sailor collar, Elsa's hand-made uniform expressed only practicality. Evalyn owned no such attire. Just taking off her shoes and walking in the sand seemed to her an extravagance that pushed the bounds of her professional station as a teacher. Agnes never joined the teacher and children on the beach, and Evalyn had difficulty imagining her sporting a frock similar to her daughter's and splashing about with enjoyment. Erik had no need to change for swimming; he just kept on his everyday knee-length pants and cotton shirt.

Evalyn waited for disapproval of the swimming outing to show on Agnes' face or in her countenance. It did not appear. Instead, Agnes helped the children dress in their swimming clothes and spoke in Swedish words of caution, presumed Evalyn, as Elsa and Erik nodded in unison and responded, "Yes, Mama."

Evalyn realized while walking down the beach, as Elsa and Erik ran to a clear sloping area free of oyster shells, that she filled not only the role of their teacher, but as nanny as well. She decided she did not mind. She had not tired of the children during the eight months of employment as their educator, and she felt she would have done anything for and with them. If Agnes continued to maintain stability, and no alarming incidents forced Evalyn from the Larsson's employ, she imagined she would enjoy teaching them for many years.

No waves existed on the shoreline. Barely noticeable was the water's entrance and exit onto the sand. The swash was a whisper as it flowed forward and a hush as it rescinded. From Morris Island to the shores of Sullivan's, the water was a giant mirror on its side. How could a sea have so many facets? A peril one moment and a lull another. How wide-eyed and agape the children would be if she were to walk upon the surface, thought Evalyn, fancifully.

She stopped far from the water's edge and stared at the stillness. The children giggled as they pulled off their leather shoes.

Realizing splashing about might frighten flounder, they decided to try to catch one before swimming. They looked to Evalyn for approval.

"Smart choice."

They worked together. Elsa fished around in a small pail and handed Erik a minnow caught earlier off the dock. With a metal hook, he ran it through along its tiny top fin. The hook and a small weight were tied to a long twine, which was tied to a smooth bamboo pole. Erik tossed out the twine and backed up slowly to allow the baited hook to drag through a shallow section of the shore and capture the attention of a flounder, camouflaged against the brown sand.

A jolt, as solid as if a giant footstep had trod upon the sand, perked Evalyn from her contemplation and silenced the children's glee. The body of water between the two islands' shorelines became a massive ripple that started with a small circle and continued swiftly into a series of concentric circles that eventually dissipated as they reached each shore's edge.

"What was that?" called Erik, the bamboo pole motionless in front of him.

Elsa ran to Evalyn's side. She grabbed her teacher's hand and looked into her face to find answers.

Evalyn stared out at the water and then toward the marsh and surrounding forest. She turned and looked back toward the lighthouse and strained to hear a warning sound from Lias. The sea regained its composure, and no wind disrupted a single leaf or needle.

"Hmm. I'm not sure. Maybe there is one of those quick storms over on James and a lightning bolt hit a tree."

"But we could see black clouds from here if there were any," offered Erik, still holding the pole and looking around.

"Not if they are tucked closer to Charleston." Then she smiled reassuringly. "It's okay. Finish fishing. Or, swim." She released Elsa's hand. "Go now! Enjoy! Summer is soon over!"

Elsa looked at Erik. Apprehension disappeared.

"I don't want to fish!" announced Elsa. "Let's swim now."

Erik rolled his eyes and began wrapping the twine around the pole. Elsa ran by him. "Last one in is a slimy jelly fish!"

"No fair!"

Sand sprayed behind Elsa's heels. She hit the water face first. Erik threw down the pole and followed her. He spun and landed in the water on his back.

The scene, thought Evalyn, was one of childhood happiness. She was pleased with how clearly her students were speaking English, even in their casual conversations.

The children eased back into an excited state. Their splashing and jumping soon disrupted the water's former stillness. Water sprayed around them.

Evalyn, poised at the water's edge, smiled when the children looked her way. But the disruptive jolt to the late August day's tranquility had caused a shift in her spirit. She looked toward James Island and then out to sea and then back again at the lighthouse. Nothing stirred. All was quiet.

What could it have been?

She was turning toward the marsh forest when Elsa yelled, "Miss Gray!"

Evalyn wheeled around to see the water receding rapidly that only seconds before had been around the children's waist. Evalyn's eyes darted farther down the shoreline. She realized water was being sucked by some invisible force away from the island and out of the channel and into the ocean beyond. Within a few blinks, the children were standing on wet sand, with no water even pooled at their feet. A nearby flounder flapped violently, obviously surprised by the sudden disappearance of its habitat. Gripped by the phenomenon, Elsa and Erik froze. Erik watched the water's quick retreat, while Elsa stared wide-eyed at Evalyn.

"Come children! Hurry now!" She ran toward the shoreline and grabbed for Elsa's hand. She managed to pick up their shoes with the other hand and began walking rapidly in the direction of the house. Erik grabbed the fishing pole and followed closely behind. At first, Evalyn maintained a steady and controlled pace, but she broke into a run upon seeing the house. Her grip tensed around Elsa's small hand.

"What's happening?" Elsa shrilled.

"I'm not sure. Let's just get back." Evalyn tried to keep panic from invading her words.

Just as they reached the edge of the line of forest, before becoming fully exposed by anyone inside the house, Evalyn stopped. She glanced back at the sea. A gasp escaped her chest. She instinctively yanked Elsa and Erik behind her. The ocean was spitting back at the shoreline a barreling wave – a line of foam and fury. The retreating water only moments earlier was hurrying toward land.

Evalyn turned back toward the house to see Lias running toward them. With one arm he swept Elsa up and led the charge not toward the house, but the lighthouse. As he ran, he shouted in the direction of the house: "Agnes! Agnes!" His entreaty followed with something in Swedish. He yanked open the lighthouse door. As he did, he looked back at the beach. Instead of entering the lighthouse, the four stood rapt to watch the watery wall, three times the height of their picket fence, flow forcefully onto the entire expanse of the beach and up into the forest. Then the backwash slinked gradually into place at the shore's edge, and a procession of insignificant rolling waves began a natural rhythm along the beach as if nothing disruptive had just occurred. The slope of the beach had diverted the giant wave away from the house and lighthouse.

"What just happened?" asked Erik.

"Did you feel the boom?" followed Elsa.

"Yes. And I understand nothing of what is happening," responded their father, who still held open the lighthouse door. "I am glad you are safe. I receive message from across ... from Sullivan's. They not understand boom. No storms nearby. Sea too calm. I see water leave beach. And then, this ..." Suddenly he whispered, "Agnes."

He let go of the heavy lighthouse door, which made a loud clank as it slammed shut. He hurried toward the house and then stopped. Lias turned back toward Evalyn and his children who had stepped in line behind him. "Let me check on her first. Say nothing to her. Perhaps she hears nothing … sees nothing. We not worry her. Yes?" They all nodded in agreement and followed him to the house. "Children, change your clothing. Miss Gray, please …"

"I will go upstairs."

"Yes."

When they entered the home, they all understood immediately – without needing to speak a word – why Agnes may not have heard or seen the peculiar goings on. She was cranking the handle on the copper wash tub, which made an awful racket while the agitators rose up and down to pound the soap and water into the clothing. Just as loud were the rotating gears on the wringer. Washing day took time, and the contraption clanked with each turn of the handle.

Evalyn lingered before making her way upstairs. The washroom door was open and she noticed Agnes start as Lias entered. Relief manifested clearly in Lias' carriage when he realized his wife's oblivion of the worrisome events transpiring outdoors. Evalyn doubted Agnes noticed her husband's relief, but an ache roused in Evalyn. She suspected the outwardly stoic man must bear within a great burden concerning his mentally fragile spouse.

The afternoon was free of odd incidents. Occasionally, while the children's heads bowed to their reading and slates, Evalyn glanced out the window, beyond the lighthouse to the horizon, and up the beach. Nothing anomalous appeared or was felt. Evalyn felt strange even thinking about it, as if it was part of last night's dream she simply could not shake. But it had happened, and the children and Lias must be swirling in their thoughts as well.

After finishing the laundry, Agnes pulled a chair to the table, and without a word to her children or their teacher took a piece of paper from the small pile at the table's center and began to write – as was becoming her daily custom.

"Shall we write to each other?" asked Evalyn. "The book instructs that formal letter writing is …"

"No!" Agnes looked up, a steel point pen suspended over the paper. "I write to … No! I not do that." Her declaration emphatic, she went back to writing.

The children looked to Evalyn for guidance. She smiled and continued: "Let's pretend, Erik, that you are the local magistrate ... remember what a magistrate is?"

"Yes, Miss Gray."

"And Elsa, you are a widow who needs help understanding how to sell part of her property. Just a sentence or two to him and then he will write you back. Let's practice writing the different parts of the letter ... the heading and the correct greeting, and then the body, and finally the closing."

Agnes ignored Evalyn's instructions to the children and wrote intensely, scratching harshly her pen across the paper. The lines on her face intensified as she wrote; at no time did she pause to ask either of her children advice or spelling questions.

Elsa finished proudly her few sentences to the "magistrate;" Erik filled in the heading on his paper, leaving space for his reply to "the widow." Elsa folded the paper, and with a grin she walked outside and came back in to announce, "A letter for you, Magistrate Larsson." Erik rolled his eyes and snatched the letter from her. Elsa giggled. Evalyn smiled, satisfied that the children could learn through role playing. Erik quickly wrote his reply, checked it, and with a mischievous grin, copied Elsa's actions: folding the letter, leaving the home, and then returning with the announcement of "mail delivery."

All the while, Agnes showed no sign of recognizing her children's amusement. After about 20 minutes of frantic writing, she rose abruptly. From the pantry and back-of-the-house kitchen emanated the sounds of cabinet doors opening and closing and an occasional pot lid clanking.

Lias hurried in just before the supper hour to remind Agnes that a little food needed to be set aside for the lighthouse-keeper-in-training, a Richard Stonebridge. He was taking inventory and settling in at the Life Saver Station, double checking supplies to make ready for the oncoming hurricane season, but he would not be taking an evening meal with the Larssons, explained Lias. Perhaps they would meet him the following day, Lias mentioned to the children, who appeared eager to meet anyone new visiting their isolated island habitat. Lias sat at the dining table only long enough to politely clean his plate, and then announced that he must take food and a few toiletries to Mr. Stonebridge before retreating to evening sentry duties within the great lighted tower.

Lias took the tea-towel wrapped bundle of food from Agnes and thanked her. As Agnes exited the dining room to return items to the pantry, Evalyn rose impulsively and followed Lias into the entryway. Later she would wonder why her characteristic thoughtful nature eluded her at that moment. It was not a planned act. Earlier forebodings had aggravated her consciousness all through the afternoon.

"I just want to know if anything else has happened?" she blurted, perhaps a little too loudly. "I cannot stop thinking about it … it doesn't make sense. I just wonder …"

When Lias turned to meet her, Evalyn grasped in his manner the carelessness of her actions: his so-slight head shake, the discomfited way he dipped his chin and diverted his eyes, and the "good night, Miss Gray" muttered under his breath as he opened the door and exited the home. For a moment she stood still, staring at the closed door, penetrated through by the eyes she knew burned directly behind her. Evalyn turned to meet Agnes' glare full on.

"Mrs. Larsson, I …"

But Agnes turned back toward the dining room, snapping in Swedish at Elsa, who nervously collected dishes from the table.

Weighted with her blunder, Evalyn paused at the stairwell and listened to what she thought must be an interrogation in Swedish. Elsa's voice grew thin as she attempted to explain "Miss Gray's" statement. Erik walked in from collecting water for cleaning dishes and caught Evalyn eavesdropping — even though inflection and tone, not words, were all that her mind could comprehend. "Mama's wondering what 'happened' today," translated Erik in a whisper.

"I thought so," responded Evalyn. "I am so, so sorry. I am not certain what came over me."

"No worries. Yes?" said Erik, exhibiting the assured strength of his father.

With a full pail in each hand, he approached his mother and sister and spoke calmly, but Evalyn noted a pointed quality in his voice. Agnes' harsh questioning ceased and all that could be heard as Evalyn ascended the stairs was the tinkle of porcelain touching porcelain and the scuffing of shoe leather against hardwood flooring.

Evalyn retired for the evening without knowing what Erik said to assuage his mother's concern. Whatever it was, it lasted only a few hours.

******

"Miss Gray!"

Evalyn glanced at the wall clock – 9:25. She disrupted *An Essay on Studies in Hysteria and the Case of Anna O* as she jumped up from the bed. The booklet fluttered to the floor, pages open. Since retiring for the evening, a stone had weighed in her gut at the thought of Agnes unraveling due to the clumsy comment earlier. She had decided to read more of the essay to try to prepare. For what, she was not certain.

"Come quickly," yelled Erik from the stairwell.

Evalyn slid her feet into bedside slippers and grabbed for her muslin covering, wrapping it around her gown while bounding down the stairs. In the dining room, Agnes stood, trance-like, facing the far wall. In her hand was the spring-load mechanical pencil from Evalyn's school supply box, housed daily in a top drawer of the room's oak buffet. Agnes was writing on the wall. Spread across the dining table were sheets of paper with words scrawled largely; some of the paper was crumpled. Elsa stood at the doorway, face in hands, whimpering softly. On three of the room's four walls were words, as high up as Agnes could reach. Evalyn tried to make them out in the room lit dimly by the fading August sun and a kerosene lantern.

"I've tried talking to her, but she won't answer," said Erik.

"Your Papa still inside the lighthouse?"

"Yes."

"Mrs. Larsson." Evalyn moved a few steps toward the table to try to read some of the words on the paper. They were in Swedish. "Mrs. Larsson, can I get you something?"

Agnes scribbled furiously on the back wall; no acknowledgment showed in her countenance. As Evalyn approached, she tried to remember Freud's cautions regarding hysteria.

"Mrs. Larsson," Evalyn said louder, while also trying to avoid a sharpness in her tone. She moved to the wall closest to the dining room's entry door to get a better look at the writing. Some of the words were in English. *No more dark. No more dark. No more dark.* The English words, written over and over again, were sandwiched horizontally between lines in Swedish.

Agnes continued to write, filling wall space at a frantic pace.

"Erik," whispered Evalyn, motioning for him to come closer. "What does this say?"

Erik sidestepped toward his teacher, glancing warily at his mother on the other side of the dining table. He translated: "*What else* has happened? *What else has happened? It is coming. It is coming.* And then some other words …" He paused. "I do not think they are words."

Erik pointed to one Swedish word, which was written repeatedly below the English lines from about waist height to the wall's baseboards. Hills and valleys of scribblings. "Light," he said. "*Ljus* means light."

"Mama," Erik pleaded, walking slowly toward his mother. "Let us help you."

Evalyn, still studying the wall, whirled. She remembered a clear warning from Freud: *Do not attempt to antagonize or disturb a person who is experiencing a hysteric trance.*

"Erik, no!"

His soft touch to his mother's shoulder was an electric shock. She swung around and thrust the pencil into her son's flesh, just below the clavicle. He did not scream. That is what Evalyn remembered most about the incident. Erik looked into his mother's wild eyes and then at the pencil protruding from his body. But Agnes screamed. She screamed the same primal scream elicited at the James Island picnic. She yanked the pencil out of her stunned son, leaned against the wall, slid down, wrapped her arms around her knees, and began to moan and sway.

Evalyn ran into the pantry and grabbed a cloth. Erik stumbled out of the dining room and into the stairwell, where Elsa sat on the first step sobbing loudly. Evalyn grabbed Erik's and Elsa's arms and pulled them forcefully into their bedroom. She slammed the door, turned the key in the lock, and dropped it into a pocket in her gown. She had them sit on the edge of one of the beds and applied pressure to Erik's wound. Dabbing at the water in the basin by the bed, she wiped at blood that seeped onto his cotton nightshirt; she lifted the fabric to clean the skin. In the light of their room's kerosene lamp, which glowed low, indicating need for more oil, Evalyn could not determine if the lead had broken off in Erik's soft tissue. Elsa continued to cry, and Erik's body began to shake. Evalyn draped the cloth over the basin and knelt down in front of them. She pulled them toward her and held them, whispering, "I am so sorry. Please forgive me."

"It is not your …" started Erik.

A brilliant light unexpectedly illumined the room. It was not the powerful and far-reaching Fresnel lens light that gave hope to far-off sailors and reminded Charlestonians and sea-islanders of the lighthouse's steady existence. This light's intensity, though it remained for only a few seconds, transfixed the room's occupants. Harsh day-like light; then night again.

Elsa's cries were immediately arrested. Evalyn pulled back from the children, her mouth agape.

"What is happening, teacher?" whined Elsa, as the room's low lamp-lit glow returned.

Another scream emanated from the dining room, and then the stairwell. Evalyn scrambled toward the door and pushed a heavy chest, situated at the foot of Elsa's bed, in front of the locked door. But the next sound they heard was the home's entryway door being opened and closed, and Agnes' screams faded in the direction of the beach. Evalyn gathered the children close to her on the bed and held their quivering bodies.

"Papa ... I want Papa," cried Elsa for several minutes, while Evalyn kept one arm around her and used her other hand to apply pressure to Erik's wound. She lifted the towel often to evaluate the blood flow.

As if he heard his daughter's tearful summons, Lias began pounding at the door. "Agnes?" He rattled the handle. "Open!"

Evalyn released her hold on the children and pushed the barricade away from the door.

"Agnes!" Lias yelled impatiently. "Erik! Elsa!"

"Just one moment," responded Evalyn, feeling in her gown's pocket for the key.

"Papa!" cried Elsa.

"Is everyone safe? Why is door locked?" A stern rebuke in Swedish followed.

Evalyn fumbled with the key, her hand shaking.

"Coming Papa," assured Erik.

Evalyn unlocked the door and Lias burst into the room. In the diminishing light, he sought the faces of his family. Elsa flung herself into his waiting arms and grasped him tightly around the neck. He looked past her for Agnes. "Where is ..."

"Oh, Papa ..." started Erik.

Lias' eyes widened at the sight of blood on his son's nightshirt.

"Erik! What has hap ..."

"She has run out into the night," interrupted Evalyn.

"What? Agnes? But Erik … the blood?"

"There has been much difficulty this evening, I'm afraid," she said, trying to maintain some restraint. "Erik tried to help … she … I am so sorry … my worries to you earlier … my comment …" Evalyn's wall crumbled; she fell to her knees, her white gown pooled around her. Her face fell into her lap and she cried.

"Miss Gray. Miss Gray, please." Lias knelt beside Evalyn, wrapped his expansive arms around her and Elsa, and grabbed at his son's shirt sleeve to pull him into the shelter.

"Son, are you …" Lias tried again.

"It's my fault," managed Evalyn., wiping with a sleeve the flow of water and mucus on her face. "I have treated his small wound. He will be fine. The light, she ran …"

"The light was a comet in sky … I run down stairs when see it because I think of Agnes, … it will scare …"

At first the movement was faint, but all four felt it at the same time. Elsa clutched Lias' arm tighter as he pulled her up and took a standing position. Evalyn rose slowly as the ground beneath them buckled and – as everyone within a 100-mile radius would later describe – waved. Wooden floorboards strained perceptibly. And as the waves intensified, they were followed by a severe shaking motion that resulted immediately in a deafening roar accompanied by the sounds of breaking glass and china, crashing furnishings, and buckling floor joists.

Lias bellowed, "Outside!" When he turned to usher them out, he saw that Agnes stood in the doorway, stone-faced, staring at them.

"Agnes! Run!"

He pushed them along. Elsa stumbled and fell to her knees. Erik grabbed her waist and half dragged her. Agnes bounded, crazed and rabbit-like, to the left and then the right. The ground was a tempest, rising and dipping as they dashed blindly away from the house and lighthouse.

Evalyn remembered nothing as clearly about their frenzied nighttime dash to safety except the deafening roar that seemed to her to occupy the air's every molecule. She had no idea why there would have been a roar, but newspapers later reported survivors sharing the same curious description.

When they were on the marsh side of the house, closest to the creek, but away from the beach, the jarring under their feet ceased, abruptly. An unnatural silence engulfed the previously wracked space. Until Agnes screamed. Her clear expression of torment panicked

Evalyn far more than what she thought was the destruction of the world.

Lias grabbed his wife's arms and spoke sternly to her in Swedish. She looked at him and tried to pull away, to run. The anger in his alarm overcame him and he yanked her forcefully to the ground, yelling again in Swedish. He pointed his finger at her and yelled again. The screaming stopped and she submitted, slowly rolling over onto her side in the sand and curling into a fetal position. Elsa stood straight and cried; Erik wrapped an arm tight around her and looked at his father for guidance. The only light illuminating the strange night was the Fresnel's continuous rotation.

"Are you hurt?" Lias asked Evalyn. She could barely make out his face in minimally lit darkness, but his voice communicated excruciation.

"I am not hurt," answered Evalyn, who stood close to the children. The horrors of the night seeped in.

"Children?"

"Fine, Papa," answered Erik for them both.

Lias reached out, and the light revealed only momentarily his hand as it brushed over both their heads. Agnes remained still at his feet. He appeared uncertain. Evalyn watched him in the sporadic light as he looked toward the lighthouse, at his children, down at the futile form at his feet, and then back at the lighthouse. He started to speak but was interrupted by a far-off sound that grew and accelerated. It came from the direction of James Island and even farther beyond: Charleston. It was Dante's 6th level of hell made audible. A shrieking and moaning ascended and then rained down around them.

In the passing light, Evalyn saw Agnes – a woman-child curled on the humid ground – bring hands to cover her ears. The children edged closer to their father and leaned in. As he strained to understand the elevating noise, Evalyn too drew closer. Still standing over his wife, Lias seized tightly Evalyn's hand and curled his other arm around his children. They all looked in the direction of the din. A glow radiated in the distance. At first a faint yellowish hue, and then a horizon like the sinking sun.

"Charleston!" whispered Evalyn. "It's burning."

While they stood, paralyzed, watching the glowing line, the earth began again to express its force. A great being arched its back under their feet. Evalyn, whose hand was still absorbed into Lias', clutched his forearm with her other hand. The children screamed and cried. Lias' mass grew as he hovered protectively, bracing himself as if against a mighty wind. In the midst of the suffocating noise of groaning earth and far-off dismayed and suffering persons, tall, branchless palms along the forest's edge cracked and thwacked the sandy ground. And then the circling light revealed what their ears heard first: a cannon blast of liquid shot straight into the air just in front of the marsh – not 50 yards from where they stood. Mud and gas and brackish water splattered back to earth: the sound, a herd of galloping horses. Blobs of warm earthen goo hit the party. Evalyn screamed and Lias in one swift movement grabbed Agnes up from her hunkered state. Interwoven bodies as one moved again, this time hurriedly toward the boardwalk closest to the marsh pier.

Once more, the jarring stopped. But not the noise. Charleston's agony reverberated around them.

Elsa fainted onto the sandy grass. Lias picked her up, his chest heaving from fright. Erik cried out, "Elsa!" He tugged at his father's sleeve.

"Elsa will awaken. It is better she … I know not … I …" He sought his breath. "Your wound!" The lighthouse light intensified Erik's blood-stained nightshirt.

Agnes stood a few feet away, the whites of her eyes large and luminous in the intermittent darkness. She stared at her son, her husband, her unconscious daughter.

Evalyn sought answers and protection in Lias' face, but his eyes bulged from distress.

Lias panted for a few moments before he spoke. "It is earthquake, I believe. I know not where is best place to be. The house … lighthouse, not safe." He looked at his wife, who stood ghost-still staring at him. "Agnes." He reached out a hand underneath his cradled daughter. "We stay here, dear." He motioned for her to come close to him. "We wait here." His voice transitioned into a Swedish plea and he took a step toward Agnes, his daughter still motionless in his arms. Agnes stepped backward and spoke only a few words in Swedish, turning while she did so and pointing to the light.

"No!" Lias managed, the ground swelling again beneath them.

Agnes began running and disappeared just as the light swirled around toward the sea.

The shock wave roused Elsa; Lias dumped her into Erik's arms and pushed them to the ground. He yelled to the children in Swedish and they clutched one another. "Stay with them!" he shouted to

Evalyn. He, too, vanished into the darkness. An infernal drum beat around them. Evalyn strained to see Agnes and Lias as the light whirled toward the space between house and lighthouse. She caught sight of him just as he disappeared inside the steel lighthouse door. Kneeling next to the whimpering children, she stroked their hair. "Mama! Papa!" they cried. The earth stilled again. Evalyn kissed their heads and drew them close. Every time the light exposed the space in front of the lighthouse door, she expected to see Lias exiting with Agnes. She prayed for their safety, for the stability of the tall structure, for impending danger to end. Seconds and minutes dragged. Then a muffled but echoing shriek startled Evalyn to her feet.

"Stay here, children!"

"No!" she heard them wail behind her as she ran furiously toward the lighthouse. Down the beach she could see a light bumping along toward her. She had forgotten about Mr. Stonebridge. She did not wait for him but pulled open the monstrous door. Thick darkness. Footsteps clanked on metal above her. She stood in the doorway, holding the door open. She looked up into dark nothingness. A pinprick of the twirling light from outside penetrated momentarily an upper window. Evalyn caught the movement of Lias at least 10 flights up. All she heard were his heavy booted feet as he descended rapidly. She could see nothing inside the doorway. She let go of the door and felt for the lighthouse wall as Lias drew nearer.

"Where's Agnes?" she yelled, as she took a step forward. One of her leather-bottomed slippers slid into a heap on the floor. She startled backward. At the same time, the entryway flooded with light, Lias reached the bottom stair, and Mr. Stonebridge shrieked, "Dear God in heaven!"

The light from the lantern Mr. Stonebridge carried reflected off the red and growing pool that haloed around Agnes' head.

THE AFTERMATH

Since the earthquake, Evalyn had managed to find and read editions of newspapers printed a few days before and the morning of. She reread the article from the weekend prior to the earthquake about the "disturbance" on the roof and in the cellar that awakened a couple. She remembered Lias mentioning that Agnes woke him and spoke of a disturbance as well. Evalyn read over and over again how others, especially residents of Summerville, the earthquake's epicenter, noted to news-hungry journalists many days before the actual earthquake of trees moving, doors slamming, and shutters banging – without the benefit of wind. One eloquent journalist wrote on August 29: "A young man describes that he felt that he had been grabbed by the neck, turned topsy-turvy against his will, and then became slightly nauseated."

By the 30th, the word "earthquake" and "shock" appeared subtly as possible reasons for the odd sounds and unexplained movements. But naysayers were quick to decry these reported insinuations as figments of imaginations or doomsday accounts by the overly spiritual.

Evalyn noticed in her limited research that a small headline on the 30th announced "The Earthquake in Augusta" less than 200 miles away. But there was no panic. The article led with "A slight but distinct of earthquakes was felt in Augusta yesterday morning." No one appeared to have been injured, and more than a few people thought that their homes were being invaded by robbers or, as one man told the reporter, "murderers."

On the morning of August 31, 1886, all appeared staid. The Bank of Charleston shared its report on a capital sum of $200,000 and undivided profits of $90,000. James Allan & Co. on Kings Street advertised watches, opera glasses, jardinières, and bric-a-brac. And "Leadership in England," dominated the front page of the *Charleston News and Courier.*

Also reported, up until the 31st, were sulfur smells emanating in various spots in and around the 24 miles from Summerville to Charleston. Some people claimed nausea and sickness due to the unexplained rotten-egg-like vapors.

When added up and taken as a whole, after the fact, warnings were clear of an impending and catastrophic event. But historical accounts since the British "founding" of Charleston in 1670 documented only a "rumbling" or a "slight shock" in 200 years. Newspapers were adamant that in two centuries, nothing seismic of any consequence had occurred or even threatened the lowcountry, so how could citizens have prepared. Even attentive scientists shared how embarrassingly unprepared they were for August 31.

But Agnes knew. Fragile mental health resulted in a sensitivity and perceptiveness that eluded others, thought Evalyn.

Sequestered in her home, Evalyn had nothing to do but read – and cry.

The September 1st headline attempted to capture the event in a few words: "A Terrible Earthquake – Charleston Shaken from Centre to Circumference." The article read as something from a sensational and fictional novel: "An earthquake such as has never been known in the history of this city, swept over Charleston last night causing more loss to injury and property and far more loss of life than the cyclone of the year before. The city is wrecked."

Queen Victoria's published telegraph to President Grover Cleveland from Balmoral Castle in Scotland, three days after the quake, elevated briefly survivors' fortitude.

I desire to express my profound sympathy with the sufferers by the late earthquakes, and await with anxiety fuller intelligence, which I hope may show the effects to have been less disastrous than reported. The Queen

President Cleveland's response from the Executive Mansion in Washington demonstrated his concern: *Your majesty's expression of sympathy for the sufferers by the earthquake is warmly appreciated and awakes grateful response in American hearts.*

Evalyn noticed that reporters also made much ado about Clara Barton's visit to Charleston. The Civil War heroine and Red Cross Society president doled out $500 for medical relief efforts. In the bedlam, austere men overlooked Barton's feminism, conveying clearly their appreciation for the needed funds.

Charleston had in one night become a tent city of thousands of souls. Classes and races stirred together in a survival pot. The earthquake had eliminated all pretention. White and black bodies wailed and wandered, often clad only in night clothes and dressing gowns soiled with smoke, blood, dirt, and sweat. The crying and shrieks and loud prayers and exhortations had continued unabated into the following morning, but they ebbed and flowed for more days as bodies were discovered and aftershocks continued. Broken bones, gashes, spinal injuries, and burns were the result of falling façades, bricks, plaster, and whole buildings as well as fires from disrupted gas lines, candles, and lanterns. Some managed to make it out of buildings during the initial quake, only to be injured or killed from compromised buildings that tottered and fell after the subsequent shocks. By the morning of September 1, at least 100 human lives, and countless horses, cows, dogs, cats, chickens, and swine had succumbed to the previous evening's catastrophes. Flight had been the only salvation, and birds had taken to the star-dense night and remained unscathed.

A September 3 commentary shared, "The catastrophe which has befallen Charleston lacked nothing in the elements necessary to make it appalling, not only on account of the terrible loss of life and the widespread destruction of property, but because of the suddenness of the stroke and its wholly unique character. It was not only an overwhelming calamity, but a new and strange one." The journalist went on to philosophize about how people were used to tornadoes and hurricanes, but left reeling all the more from a mysterious natural disaster that catapulted them instantly from "peace and calm" to the "horrors of the unexpected and unknown."

Survivors rued their comfortable past and concentrated on the basics: food, water, medical attention, and shelter (preferably not one that would fall on them as the result of an aftershock). People who had never known anything but a comfortable bed and down pillow slept on the ground in open parks and vacant lots.

Though a listing of detailed and gruesome accounts dominated papers on the following day and days thereafter, nothing seemed to compare to the nightmare from which Evalyn thought she would not rouse.

Yet, column after column exposed the affected and their misfortunes:

- Ellen Mitchell, mulatto, serious internal injuries, residence Judge Bryan's yard

- Mr. J.C.E. Richardson, seriously injured in the head by his house falling in upon him, condition very critical

- Isaac Jenkins, colored, wall fell on him in cow alley, seriously damaged all over body

Although Summerville was officially the epicenter, Evalyn discovered that most residents of the small rural town were spared the earthquake's violence. Their compromised simple, single-floor clapboard homes threatened few injuries, unlike the crumbling and collapsing multi-storied brick and stucco structures in nearby Charleston.

Many families, who annually escaped summer's heat by retreating to their mountainous Flat Rock second homes, were traveling the evening of August 31st by train through Summerville on their way into Union Station on East Bay Street in Charleston when they experienced a tumultuous 60 seconds. Charles Wesley, a passenger with his mother and younger sister, composed himself enough afterwards to share with a reporter: "We seemed to pitch suddenly forward and down, as if falling into a hole. And then the engine rose upward as if climbing a hill. We leveled out and rode of all of maybe three seconds in a curvy 'S' formation before our car and the engine jumped the tracks, bumped cruelly on the bare ground, and then halted, teetered, and fell onto its side." Clamoring and bewildered passengers managed to climb out of windows and opened doors. They were scratched and bruised, but the engineer and firemen experienced graver wounds. The next day, the paper shared that the train track was frozen in bended waves.

In each newspaper, Evalyn searched for news about the lighthouse's fate, and any mention of Agnes' death, Lias' arrest, or her own interrogation. She gathered little; there were only slight allusions reported.

On September 4 she found: "The Morris Island lighthouse was injured by the earthquake. A portion of the tower is cracked. The light, however, has been kept burning every night. The beacons sustained no damage." A published Coast Guard report indicated that although the giant Fresnel lens was "thrown out of position," both it and the "broken parts of the tower" were in the process of being mended "without delay." A working Morris Island lighthouse, though it would no longer be cared for and operated by Lias Larsson from Sweden, was essential, conveyed the article. A city in disarray did not mean its harbor would for very long discontinue business as usual.

Newspapers were vague on why "Keeper Larsson" was no longer at the helm, other than to express that the earthquake had caused an "accident" that was under investigation by the Coast Guard. Another keeper was called in to maintain the light. Such business might have been sensationally newsworthy during quieter times, but all entities of Charleston's media, law enforcement, and the medical community had their hands full. What had happened on Morris Island would have to wait to make headlines at a later date.

Evalyn learned more about earthquakes than she cared to know. Possessing always a teacher's mind, she thought fleetingly yet longingly of how Elsa and Erik would benefit from her sudden knowledge of the term "seismic" and how the energy of Charleston's earthquake was significantly higher than anything previously recorded on the East Coast. She wondered who, if anyone, was sharing information about the disaster with the children. Were they being kept in the dark about their parents? She stifled another, of numerous, sobs at the idea that they must be among strangers. Evalyn imagined their mother's body had been prodded, examined, and even photographed by Coast Guard investigators, and their father most likely sat alone in a well-guarded tent somewhere on Morris Island, or on James. Or perhaps they held him in the hold of a ship anchored just off the coast.

The moments and hours after the main earthquake and the shocks that followed, and after Agnes' death, were simultaneously a blur or razor sharp in Evalyn's consciousness. She felt numb and nauseous one minute and restless the next. On the night of the 31st, a panicked, perplexed Mr. Stonebridge had thrown a loaded pistol, a flair gun, and first-aid kit into a canvas bag and run down the beach toward the lighthouse. In his horror of seeing Agnes' body on the lighthouse floor and her skull cracked and bleeding, and upon finding Evalyn standing over Agnes and Lias frozen on the bottom step, the already traumatized Mr. Stonebridge had groped nervously in the bag for the pistol and pointed it at Lias, then at Evalyn, and then back at Lias.

Although Evalyn had not officially been arrested, she was carried off the island the next day by members of the Coast Guard, who Mr. Stonebridge had signaled immediately with the flair gun after tying Lias at gunpoint to a boardwalk pillar. Head down, Lias had consented pitiably.

Initially, a shaking Mr. Stonebridge had ordered Evalyn and the children to sit out the rest of the terrifying night in the yard to the left side of the house, several yards away from Lias. Mr. Stonebridge stood over Lias, pistol held taut in one hand, and waited for dawn and for Coast Guards to relieve him and make sense out of the woman lying at the base of the lighthouse.

Elsa and Erik had cried intermittently and clutched their teacher through the night. Their grasp tightened each time a new shock occurred. Charleston's distant but perceptible anguish continued unabated. Shocked and dazed mute from the baffling horrors, the children had not asked about the whereabouts of their mother or the reason for their father's restraints until the morning light revealed what the darkness shielded from them.

"Why is Papa tied?" whimpered Elsa. "*Papa!*"

Lias had not lifted his head.

"Your Mama ... she, she ... fell in the lighthouse last night," whispered Evalyn, hardly believing the words that spilled from her mouth.

Elsa gasped. Erik stared across the yard at his father and did not speak.

"Is she ...?" cried Elsa. "*Mama!*"

"I am not sure how she is." Evalyn had lied and stroked the blond hair; her gown was wet from the children's tears. "Mr. Stonebridge is taking care of your Papa and he has called for help for your Mama. He is doing his duty ...," she had managed. "We must wait just a little longer."

She had considered saying more, to assure them that all would be fine – to assure them of something. But she had sat in the sandy grass, deadened from the series of unfathomable events.

But Papa … they have him tied!" cried Elsa, confused. "Why? *Papa!*"

Erik had stood up and walked, and then ran, toward his father.

"Erik, no!" yelled Evalyn.

Mr. Stonebridge, though sleep deprived and weary, had attempted to block Erik from reaching his father, but Erik darted around him and knelt down. Mr. Stonebridge protested, his gun pointing down from his right hand. Erik ignored him, faced his father, and spoke in Swedish, tears streaming. Lias had lifted his head and responded.

Evalyn heard only muffled words. A few moments passed and Erik walked heavily back to where Evalyn and Elsa sat. He slumped down, pulling his knees in close to hide his face. Elsa resumed crying into Evalyn's close embrace. Evalyn's sandy, mud-splattered, sweat-stained gown became soaked through with Elsa's salty tears.

Two boats docked by mid-morning. Two men in each boat. They tied the boats and marched officially down the pier to where Mr. Stonebridge stood over Lias. He had just retrieved water from the house and was holding a cup in front of Lias' mouth.

Evalyn could not hear what they were saying. They nodded their heads in agreement, while Lias mostly kept his head down. He looked up only once, moved his lips, and again dropped his head. The party moved to inside the entryway of the lighthouse; one of the men, younger, with his uniform hanging slouchy on his too-narrow shoulders, backed up and ran around to one side of the lighthouse, out of site. He returned, momentarily, wiping the back of his hand across his mouth. Evalyn watched as he stood outside the lighthouse door, while the others convened inside for a few moments.

When the men exited the door, each of them shaking their lowered heads, one of the officials approached Evalyn and stated, "We are going to need a statement." Another offered her and the children a cup of water and a biscuit. Then, without warning, the children were suddenly pulled off their teacher and Evalyn felt a firm grip on her arm. She was led to one of the boats. The children screamed and cried while two of the men wrapped their arms around them from behind and held them firmly in place. Evalyn had tried to turn around; she yelled, "Be brave!" Yet, in their cries, she could not be certain if they heard her. When she settled into the boat, Elsa and Erik were being pulled toward the house. Lias' head was up, and Evalyn could see —

even with the distance between them – torment tearing through him. For the first time since submitting to them, Lias wrestled with his bindings. "No! Please!"

Evalyn was taken to James Island by boat, and then assisted onto the back of a hired dock horse, which was led by one of the two men to her house. The aftershocks grew fainter as the long day wore on. Evalyn had sat numb and mostly silent on the boat and on the back of the horse. A few times the men asked questions, and she heard herself answering them, but her mind was muddled with the heft of incomprehensible events.

When she had arrived, a throng of people congregated behind the house, which – other than a porch column askew – seemed unscathed by the earthquake. The Coast Guard official led her to the doorway, blocked by a half dozen women. When they stepped aside, she saw her mother sitting on a chair. Her hair was mussed and her sobs came in harsh waves.

"Sorry to intrude, ladies," said one of the officials. "We have brought Miss Gray from Morris Island. There has been an accident. She needs to stay here." He emphasized "stay." To Evalyn he directed: "We will be back for a written statement. We have many questions. Do you understand, Miss Gray? We have many questions about what happened out there."

"Yes. I understand."

Satisfied, the men tipped their hats and left the room.

Evalyn looked around, confused. None of the women spoke. She had approached her mother and touched her gently on the shoulder. "Oh, Evalyn! He's gone! He's gone!" She had grasped her daughter's hand and held it firmly to her chest; the sobs rose shrill and dramatic.

While her mother cried, Evalyn learned from the women who crowded standing and sitting in the small home that her stepfather had been swallowed by a fissure that had cracked open a portion of earth behind the house. Still in tainted night clothes, Evalyn left her mother's side and made her way to the back of the house to a bubbling and muddy pond that existed where there was none before. She stood behind a line of men and listened.

"Near 'bout a hunderd yards, don't you think?"

"At least."

"Got the makins' of one at my place. Few shocks ago, the ground just cracked right open and sand and silt spewed forth, hittin' the trees all around and splashin' down on our roof. Touched a speck and it was downright hot. Musta' shot near 15 feet. Probably have me a muddy crater 'fore the day's over."

"What's to say we don't all get swallowed up like this poor soul?"

"Heard one took part of the negro cemetery over there near McLeod's place. Graves just sunk down farther into the earth. Least ways those souls are already dead."

"It's Armageddon, sure enough."

"What else might we see? Never, in all my years …"

"Bad way to go. Reckon' he knew what was happenin'?"

"Widow in there said they came a runnin' out when the quake hit and he run ahead of her on account of she tripped and fell with all the wavin' of the earth. It got him and the lantern. Gone! He was there one minute and then not the next."

The men stopped talking for a moment and contemplated the odd scenario. One of them turned to notice Evalyn, who stood quietly. Then the others turned. They sized up her state; their grim expressions grew grimmer.

Evalyn had peered past the men and into the wide hole, and then her gaze rested on the mud splattered trees. Two pines were down at the edge of the yard. They rested in the form of a giant cross.

"Oh, sorry miss. Sorry 'bout your daddy. He's a missin' in there somewhere."

"You okay, miss?"

"We're real sorry …"

"Sorry for your loss …"

"He wasn't my daddy," said Evalyn, and she turned and walked back to the house.

******

Within days of the earthquake, residents whose homes were partially or wholly destroyed began applying for building repair vouchers. Lists were published for all to see the extent of the workload necessary to restore Charleston. The historic city's resiliency from devastation would be tested once again, after only a less-than-two-decade hiatus. In fact, some residents on the detailed list had also applied for vouchers post-war because of what northern shells did to their dwellings. Since James and the other sea islands were substantially less damaged by the earthquake than Charleston, "cursed" was the word murmured more than once outside of Mac's, in fields, and at prayer meetings.

Chimney and roof repairs were common. Building inspectors were tasked during the following days and weeks and into months with inspecting the condition of walls, chimneys, and foundations, and determining what else needed to be done to make structures safe for the dreaded "next" earthquake many thought inevitable. Buildings badly compromised were run through with reinforcement rods. On the outside, rods were secured with bolts capped often with such adornments as stars, concentric circles, and crosses.

Almost a week after the earthquake, Evalyn was visited by more Coast Guard officials, who asked more pointed questions they said would be added to her already lengthy statement. Their tone insinuated Lias' guilt, but she took them back through the eight months of her employment to try to make them understand Agnes' precarious mental faculties. Regardless of Evalyn's forthrightness, elements of the inquiry hinted at the possibility that she may have played a part:

"What were you doing inside the lighthouse?"

"Why were you found standing over the body and not helping her?"

"What was Mr. Larsson doing with Mrs. Larsson up in the lighthouse during an earthquake?

"Did he ever tell you he and the children would be better off if Mrs. Larsson were to 'have an accident'?"

"Did you have feelings for Mr. Larsson?"

Each question was answered clearly and emphatically. She recounted excruciating details of August 31, while notes were scratched by one of the men into an official-looking journal. She suggested they interview James Islanders who witnessed Agnes' behavior at the July 4th picnic. She reiterated how she had visited a specialist in Charleston and purchased at a bookseller's the informational material on mental conditions. When she tried to explain that Agnes must have jumped, that Lias' was certainly innocent, that he loved his wife and was trying to ... – she was interrupted.

"Stick to answering the questions."

"How are the children?" she inserted, when they said they were finished but insisted they might be back with even more questions.

"That is not your business. You stay put until this whole thing is settled."

"But I care for them."

The officials ignored her and walked toward the door.

"Please ... and what of Mr. Larsson?"

"You will be informed. Do not leave this island. Good day, Miss."

THE JUDGMENT

The smell of rotting flesh drifted from the city onto the sea islands when the still-hot breezes of September wafted in their direction. A byproduct of the earthquake was not only the bodies needing burying as a direct result of the main shock and aftershocks, but many of Charleston's mostly above-ground caskets were toppled and cracked. Exposed were bodies freshly interned just days or weeks before the earthquake. Bones of the fully decomposed were jumbled and strewn throughout churches' graveyards – evidence that the earth tossed about both the living and the dead.

In poorer areas of Charleston, where families traditionally buried loved ones below ground, the earth cracked and regurgitated a great many wooden boxes. Contents that were never again supposed to see the light of day were scattered about in macabre scenes too shocking even for the heartiest of Halloween revelers.

Adding to the odor were the piles of limbs behind the hospital. While many Charlestonians kept their lives on August 31st and on subsequent days of shocks thereafter, several still lost limbs. Doctors and nurses taxed with tending the multitudes had no thought to assign someone the gruesome task of disposal. All in the city were already overwhelmed with nature's sudden upheaval of their lives.

Residents of James Island avoided the city, partly knowing more souls meant more needs, and Charleston was stretched to provide the basics for its own citizens. James Islanders shunned the hotbed of decay, where diseases – they surmised – were certain to follow. They filled their few churches and prayed, and some sent excess fall harvests to cross the Ashley River on ferries bound for the city. And they knew to keep a handkerchief at the ready when the breezes shared Charleston's unpleasant, post-earthquake smells.

Evalyn's mother, mostly despondent since the death of her husband, took to her bed when the air was particularly foul. She smothered her face in a pillow to avoid the stench and her new life. And though Evalyn asked God for forgiveness for the feeling of relief that her lewd stepfather was dead, there was the weighty realization that her mother would need her. Evalyn braced herself for a restrictive life, confined by needle and thread. She knew others' losses were potent, but she was heavy sad with her own. So many affected by the earthquake yearned to get beyond the recent trauma, but Evalyn affixed herself to it because it was the last vestige of a life she felt she may never know again. The earth shook and she was no longer the beloved teacher to two children. In an instant, one of her employers had died and the other arrested.

What would happen to the children if their father was convicted? What would happen to the three of them if he wasn't? Would she ever see any of them again? Would she have to appear in court? When would the trial occur? Evalyn sat and rocked and thought, and she tried to muster compassion for her mother. She picked up and put down and picked up again hems and patches and collars that needed attention.

"I'm going to Mac's," she called to her mother, several days after the earthquake. She dropped the skirt she had been hemming into a basket piled high with clothing articles. "I'll see if they have received any new supplies. Perhaps some rice. Collards. I heard the Anson mill is again working. They might have some fresh corn meal for cornbread."

Evalyn received no response from her mother's bedroom. She had not expected any. She grabbed her change purse, checked the pins in her hair, and started down the dirt road toward the store. She hoped getting out of the house would do her good. She hoped to learn of Lias, the date of a trial, the children.

On the way to Mac's, she decided to walk farther toward McLeod's to first visit Samuel. He had stopped by her home a few days after the earthquake to check in on her and to let her know he was not injured in the phosphate mines. Reports had communicated details of how two workers had been buried alive in one of the 10-foot pits they were working in at night to meet a fertilizer deadline.

The black death ribbon still hung on their door when Samuel had visited. He had called to Evalyn from the yard. She had stepped onto the porch and told him how relieved she was that he was safe.

Glancing at the black ribbon, he had said, "But I understand your stepfather is not."

She leaned over the porch railing and whispered, "I am glad."

Samuel had nodded his head, knowingly.

"I must not visit with you at the moment," she glanced back toward the door. "My mother … she is not handling it well."

"No. Of course. I only wanted to see for myself that you are unhurt."

Dearest Samuel.

"My body is …," she had told him, unable to say more. He had read meaning in her sad face, nodded again, and left her yard.

More than a week had transpired since his short visit. She longed to talk to him. His wisdom soothed and steadied. She was already weary from worry, from the thought of burdensome days ahead. Worry, she knew, equaled faithlessness in the very one who had answered her silent plea for safety that night, even when unimaginable chaos had rained down around them.

Evalyn approached the oak-lined entrance of McLeod's that was 25 years earlier a beacon of prosperity for the successful planter who established the property. Carriages of guests had once been in awe as they ventured down the impressive drive. But the former slaves and their descendants had transformed it into extended yards congruent to the cabins they occupied as free "citizens," since the 14th Amendment in 1868 had made them so. They worked the property for McLeod survivors and lived and were paid, to some extent, and life continued. Those who occupied the "big house" had given up on their grand entrance. A new, modest entryway was made to circle the opposite side of the property so the McLeods could approach the back of the house, which faced Wappoo Creek.

Children played and adults sang in the cotton field. An earthquake had happened, but there was no evidence at McLeod's. The fluffy white tufts bulged and broke their bolls in September and the McLeods still made some money and paid their workers' wages from the sale of the essential fiber. No trees were down; the cabins appeared intact. Evalyn did not know the three children she approached. They were playing with a few clay marbles enclosed in a circle drawn onto the dirt yard.

"Hello. Do you happen to know where Samuel is?"

One of them pointed in the direction of some trees. Another said, "graveyard."

"Thank you."

Evalyn walked away from the cotton field toward the trees just as Samuel and two other young men strode in her direction. "Samuel!"

"Evalyn!" He ran to her, wiping his hands on a torn piece of cloth. "This is Flinch and Thomas," he said when they caught up.

"Nice to meet you." Evalyn extended her hand.

"Nice to meet you, too," said Flinch, "but ma'am …"

"We're just too dang dirty," added Thomas.

Samuel smiled. "Been patchin' up the graveyard. Seems that's the only thing disturbed here. A few columns cracked at the big house and step bricks shook loose on one of the cabins. But McLeod was spared."

"Assuming the mine is closed right now?" asked Evalyn.

"Yeah. For a while at least," answered Samuel. "Helpin' around here right now, but I have something else to tell you. Goin' to wash up. Then I'll meet you in the yard."

Evalyn went back to where the children were playing marbles. Ache rose in her chest as she watched them. She considered Elsa and Erik's current state – their anxiety, fear. Had they seen their father? Had they attended the burial of their mother? Was there a service?

"So, what brings you this way?"

Evalyn took her time turning toward Samuel. He was alone. She pressed away tears lingering on her cheeks.

"Now, now … is it all bad?"

She longed to lean into her friend and allow him to embrace her. In her lifetime, that would never be possible.

"I know you must have heard what happened," she said.

"I've gotten snatches. But let me hear it from the horse's mouth."

They sat on a bench shaded at the base of one of the oaks. Evalyn relived the last few weeks, telling him of her visit to Charleston and the psychologist, the books she acquired, how the letter writing seemed to help Agnes, and then about the horrendous day and evening of the earthquake. She said simply, "I walked into the lighthouse and she was dead." Evalyn did not tell him what Agnes' body looked like or how she could not eliminate from her thoughts the image of spreading blood or of Lias' fractured expression in Mr. Stonebridge's stark lantern light. She did share how Lias was arrested and how she might be a suspect in Agnes' death.

"Is there a reason? Do they suspect there were feelings between …," tried Samuel.

"No! Oh, Samuel, no. Only compassion …of course not, nothing more," she trailed off, thinking of the few intimate moments when Lias revealed anguish over his wife's condition, when she had touched him. "He couldn't have killed her, Samuel. I believe he loved her. Even with the difficulties …"

Samuel did not respond, but his expression questioned her further. Evalyn shifted on the bench. She looked at her feet, and the two of them said nothing for a few moments.

McLeod laborers returned to the yard for a quick noon meal break of a cat-head biscuit, topped with cooked mustard greens. No one paid much attention to Evalyn and Samuel, except for a slight nod or an "Afternoon, ma'am." Workers plopped on benches in front of the cabins while some older residents served the food and some tin cups filled with water.

"Please, tell me what happened to *you* during the earthquake," asked Evalyn, desperate to shift the conversation's focus. She surprised herself by trembling slightly.

"Maybe enough is enough," said Samuel. "You seem ..."

"No. Please, go on. Your account will help take my mind off my own."

"If you're certain ..."

"Yes," she said, thankful for his concern.

He began: "I had been in the wharf warehouse. It was late, but we had been fillin' cases of the phosphate for a cargo pick up in the harbor the next day. Phosphate was still gettin' hauled in because the owners were wantin' to stock the barge full so they could make the most money. Mines were stayin' busy, even in the night. I was by myself countin' and organizin'. I had just stepped out of the warehouse with the final numbers. I don't know why, but I knew it was an earthquake right away. Heard God say, 'Hold on.' I grabbed one of the dock's pile timbers and wrapped myself 'round it. The warehouse heaved and I watched it wave up and down and then shift a full 10 feet or so to one side … but it stayed together, for the most part. Some parts of the roof crashed in though. And some lanterns hangin' around the dock fell into the water. Put me right out there in the dark. Lordy mercy, I was thankin' Him the minute it stopped. But then I heard the screamin' start."

"That was the worst part," added Evalyn. "I cannot stop hearing it in my head. We could hear it all the way out on Morris."

"It was low at first here, and then deafenin'. But what happened next was what undid me. I was standin' there tryin' to figure out what to do and fish started jumpin' up onto the dock. They were flyin' out of the water … dozens, hundreds … smackin' at me and floppin' all over the dock. I kicked at 'em to get them back in the water, but they were comin' too fast. Like the frogs and the locusts in Israel. I stepped on what I think was a ray and fell full on my back. There were too many of them … I just got off that dock and ran toward Meeting to help. Fires started and I could see then. Thought it really *was* the end. Saw two firemen grab some buckets to throw water on a burning door, and another shock … well, the house and the door buried them right in front of me. I couldn't do …"

Evalyn was deep in thought as he talked; hands clinched and rubbed in her lap as the odd and horrific events surrounding the earthquake resurfaced.

"I'm sorry, Evalyn. That's enough talk about that."

"I am fine. I suppose that our families will always suffer from memories of the war, and we will never be free of thoughts of this disaster."

"Yes, but we are not meant to stop living, are we? He spared us for a reason. We don't need to disappoint." He forced a warm smile.

"But Samuel … what could He have saved me for? I did my best out there on Morris. I even tried to help her … to help him, them. I cared for … the children. No, I loved them. I love them still … And him, their father … he cannot be guilty. He must have tried to save her. I felt alive and right and purposeful as a teacher. But it's all gone. Their lives … teaching … It's gone, Samuel." She stifled more tears and looked out toward the cotton field.

"Is it?" Samuel spoke to her softly, paternally.

"I cannot imagine leaving my mother now, and where would I teach? I have no formal training."

"Come to college with me."

"You are …"

"Yes. I have saved enough and I had decided, before the earthquake, to enroll in the fall semester. I leave in a few weeks."

"Oh, Samuel. I am so happy for you." She wanted to wrap her arms around his neck. She forced herself to sit still on the bench, her hands secure in her lap.

"I have books that you may need and can have. I no longer need them."

"Evalyn …"

"My mother …"

"You can hide the fire, but what'll you do with the smoke?"

"What?" Her tone was angry at first. Then she poked him in his ribs. "Oh, Samuel … Gullah proverbs! I am not sure what that mea …"

"You're a teacher. Nothing is going to change that. Nothing."

******

A tribunal happened without Evalyn receiving prior knowledge.

The Charleston courthouse was damaged, and people in the ravaged city were too preoccupied with their own dead to concern themselves with a death at the lighthouse. The Coast Guard decided a speedy tribunal was best. Take matters into their own hands and avoid the hoopla of a public trial. Agnes' death would eventually become a topic of conversation when the shocks forever ceased and the earthquake's newsworthiness receded in the minds of locals.

Rebuilding and restoring was foremost.

Evalyn learned after the fact that the Coast Guard had summoned keepers from Georgetown and Sullivan's Island, as well as a former keeper of Morris Island. They met for three hours in the Life Saving Station to evaluate notes from the questioning of Evalyn, a few James Islanders, Lias, and even Mr. Lundt, who admitted he had never met Agnes Larsson but shared what he could remember from the "distressed young lady" who visited him some weeks ago inquiring about her employer's "hysteria and whatnot."

Two different officers from the Coast Guard visited Evalyn "as a courtesy" to explain the tribunal's outcome.

"We are sorry we put you through an inquiry," said one, whose specks of gray hair and leathery forehead insinuated his longevity with the military branch. "Had to rule out any foul play."

"We figured Mr. Larsson was a hardened liar and a darn good actor, or he was telling the God's honest truth. 'Cause he's a downcast man over what happened to his wife," said the other, much younger officer.

"We've come to inform you that we released Mr. Larsson and your name is cleared," interrupted the older officer.

"What *did* happen?" asked Evalyn. "Did she … jump?"

"That is for Mr. Larsson to explain," stated the senior officer as he turned. "Good day, Miss Gray."

"Sir …please. Can you tell me: Where is Mr. Larsson? His children? Have they been reunited?"

"Good day, Miss," he repeated, somewhat sternly.

The younger officer lingered, hat in hand. Before turning to follow his superior, he whispered, "Paid his respects where we buried her. Got their things. Left town."

THE TOWER

The light was in front of them as they climbed the tower. Lias reached forward and grabbed Gita's hand. Though she was approaching an age when she would no longer want her Farfar to guide and protect her, or take her hand – except maybe for a moment when she married – he would do so just the same, until she otherwise objected strongly. Gita had grown up with heights. But the wooden tower was still dangerous; Lias' design for a stone one would be less so. He hoped to someday oversee such a sturdy, worthwhile project. Perhaps when the government's coffers recuperated after the war.

Gita's mother was not far behind them. She had stopped to pick the last of the wild mountain blueberries still lingering into the first days of autumn. The unusually cool summer had slowed the ripening. Gita's older brother, Zan, was miles away near Mount Mitchell finishing up his forestry certification. He was training as a lookout, but also to fight fires on the days when he was not searching for them.

"But today is your day off, is it not?" Gita asked Lias.

"Yes, but it is a beautiful day, yes? And where better to observe this beautiful day than from the tallest place? Besides, your Morsa is bringing us a picnic, remember?"

"But what about the lookout ... the one who will already be in the tower?"

"Well, I am sure Morsa remembered him, too." Lias smiled up at her. She turned and smiled back, a few of her blondish curls escaping from her bun to flow on the lofty breeze. Elsa's straight hair had married with that of her curly-headed husband's to produce Gita's enviable tresses. Elsa had become a Caird, and the Caird family immigrated from Scotland and settled amicably in the hills alongside the Cherokee, before they were forced out. Some Cherokee, hidden from soldiers by Cairds, stayed on the Caird land and were buried in the family chapel graveyard. Zan's hair was all brown curls, like his father's. No trace of Swedish showed on his head, but his jaw was square, like that of his Farfar's, and his shoulders broad as well.

Erik, having put off marriage, did not yet have children with his 20-years-younger Spanish wife. He had been too caught up researching geology and seismic activity in the hills surrounding San Francisco. What features would their blending produce in offspring, wondered

Lias. And, if children did bless them, would he ever see them? He doubted Erik would leave California and his work with other budding scientists. Erik wrote to his father of how he and a man named Richter and some "gifted" geologists were working on an instrument to detect and measure the faintest earth movements. Instead of just guessing that the earthquake that had changed all their lives had been a 6 or a 7 or even an 8 on a Mercalli scale, Erik had written passionately about finding a way to "know" exactly the power of future quakes.

Lias was proud of his son, but he missed him.

They reached the top, and as he always did, Lias warned Gita to hold onto the railing.

"Farfar! I know."

"I know that you know. But it makes me feel better to say it."

They said hello to the watchman, who offered an unsolicited rundown of activity to his superior.

"My day off, William," Lias said, smiling and patting the younger man on his shoulder.

"I won't be bothering you then."

"You're not bothering. And we will stay out of your hair. Family just wanted to come up once more before the weather turns icy. Wife's bringing a bit of a picnic up … enough to share."

"Farfar," interrupted Gita, "what are those streaming from the trees? See there, below. Those trees on the cliff line. The light is catching what looks like a single spider's thread shooting straight off the trees' branches."

"That is exactly vhat … what they are," said Lias.

"But how? Why? They can't possibly be attached to anything. Look! There are dozens of them! I can't see the ends. How do they stay so straight?"

Lias chuckled. "I am surprised your mother did not teach you … or Morsa teach you. That is not a question for me. You still want to be a science teacher?"

"Of course. What else would I be?" She turned to smile at him. "I've never wanted to be anything else but a teacher. You and Morsa know that."

"Well, when you attend college, the first question on the first day of your first semester, you must ask science professor about these spider's webs."

"Oh, Farfar! You tease so!"

"And then you must come back here during your break and teach your old grandfather."

"Will you still be teachable?"

"I hope so."

They heard voices and looked back at the tower stairs.

"Look who caught up to me," said Elsa, stepping cautiously onto the wide fire tower platform. She handed her father a basket of berries and turned to offer to take the picnic basket from Evalyn.

"Morsa! Just in time!" announced Gita. "The hike from where we tied the horses and the climb up here worked up my appetite!"

"When she is expected, Morsa comes just in time," said Elsa, winking at Evalyn, who smiled at her affectionately.

The picnic had been Elsa's idea. She had had plenty of time to suggest such an outing over the summer months. Yet, she kept busy at the Caird Farm in Franklin working alongside her husband. They had just brought in the late summer sorghum harvest and Elsa had cooked for many days prior to feed all of his extended family members who came to the all-day syrup making.

But someone had brought her the Asheville newspaper from a few days before, and she had decided to take it to show her father and Evalyn – before they learned of it on their own. The picnic in the tower was to be a distraction, in case showing them the article proved to be a bad idea.

Featured on the front of the paper, dated August 31, 1916, were first-hand remembrances of the Charleston earthquake 30 years earlier in neighboring South Carolina. The bold-faced preface introduced the Asheville reporter's account; he had been a young boy and was on a train traveling from his summer home in Flat Rock through Summerville to his family home in Charleston. Black and white photographs showed facades cut like cake slices off multi-storied buildings, of piles and piles of rubble, and of tents scattered in parks and on vacant lawns. The spread included quotes from a few older residents who lived through both the Civil War and the earthquake. And the reporter's editorializing at the end spotlighted Charleston's doggedness in times of trial, even as it held breath to learn how the great war abroad might ultimately alter its demographics. A small sidebar included a photograph of the Morris Island lighthouse and an interview with the current keeper, George Shierlock, and his wife. The keeper relayed how minor damages to the lighthouse were repaired quickly after the earthquake and how its construction was so superior as to not to have been affected in the past 30 years, even as the beach around the base rapidly eroded due to jetties built in 1898. Undoubtedly prompted by the reporter, Keeper Shierlock mentioned how when he took the job, he was informed by the keeper before him that the keeper during the earthquake had "simply disappeared" following the mysterious "never fully explained" fall and death of his wife on August 31st, 1886.

"No one knows what they could possibly have been doing up there in the lighthouse during the earthquake," was one comment, followed by: "Don't make sense. That's the last place you want to go!" Mr. Shierlock was asked his opinion on whether he thought the death an accident or murder. "I can't rightly say," he concluded, adding, "But I swear that lighthouse is haunted with Agnes Larsson's ghost. Hear a shriek sometimes, and it ain't the owls."

Elsa had read the paper, slept fitfully for a few nights, and then determined she needed to make her father and Evalyn aware of its contents. To get to the forestry service cottage occupied by Lias and Evalyn, it took Elsa about 30 minutes through a mountain gap by way of an old Cherokee road that in white society was changed to the Bartram Trail Road to honor the 18th century naturalist who explored the area. The cottage was situated on the Franklin side of the Nantahala River, and Elsa and Gita had to ride that morning their Clydesdale-cross, which had plenty of room beyond its wide withers even for a third person.

When they arrived, Elsa left the newspaper tucked in a leather pouch that hung on the saddle horn. Elsa allowed Gita to slip off the horse's back first before she dismounted herself. Folly, the shepherd mix, alerted Evalyn to Elsa and Gita's arrival. Evalyn met them in the doorway, and Elsa greeted her with a kiss to her cheek.

"This is an unexpected pleasure," Evalyn had said.

Gita had also kissed Evalyn on the cheek and then asked expectantly, "Any new books, Morsa?"

Evalyn smiled and hugged Gita. "Is that all you come here for?"

"Well, when I become a teacher like you, I'll let you borrow mine."

"Agreed."

Evalyn had been "Morsa" since she left the lowcountry and the mountains became her home almost three decades earlier. She thought it endearing that Lias reached into his Swedish past to offer up the maternal nickname, especially since he had been so determined to Americanize when she first met him. But Evalyn also realized, and appreciated, that the name retained for Agnes the distinction of "Mama" in the minds of the children.

Evalyn remembered Elsa whining so many years ago: "Not 'Miss Gray' anymore, Papa. Please!" After those first uncertain days in the Blue Ridge Mountains were behind them, and Evalyn had eventually agreed to receive Lias' hand in marriage, Elsa had declared: "She's not just our teacher now!" Erik had agreed, and the matter of addressing Evalyn as Morsa was settled. The Swedish endearment had been picked up by the grandchildren as well.

"Morsa, where is Papa?" Elsa had asked as she entered the cottage that morning.

Evalyn tilted her head toward the back of the cottage. Elsa heard her father shuffling and humming in the bedroom.

"Hello, Papa!" called Elsa.

"Hello, Farfar!" echoed Gita.

Elsa had turned to Evalyn and said in a hushed but hurried tone, "I've brought you and Papa something to look at and I'm leaving Gita for Papa to take to the tower. It *is* his day off, correct? I'm going berry picking. I thought maybe you could bring a picnic later and we'll meet up. It's been a while since we've picnicked together in the tower."

Evalyn looked curiously at Elsa. "You've brought us something?"

"Just a moment." Elsa disappeared through the front door and returned with the newspaper in her hand. She gave it to Evalyn, who had stared at the headline and then said, "Gita, the tabby's kittens opened their eyes yesterday. Check on them for me, please." Evalyn watched her granddaughter exit the front pine door.

"I don't know if I'm doing the right thing, but I just did not want you or Papa stumbling on this or hearing people talk about it," said Elsa. "I didn't want it surprising you … I know that not many people around here know what happened to us, or even realize that we were there, but I just thought you should see it this way instead of … well … getting a shock."

Evalyn stared at the headline. Dread paled further her already fair features.

"Goodness," said Elsa, regretting immediately her decision. "I'm sorry if … I just thought maybe…"

Evalyn folded the paper and forced a smile. "You are always looking out for us, Elsa. You could never do wrong by us."

Evalyn tucked the paper behind a needlepoint pillow on her rocker. She pulled Elsa close, whispering, "All is well." She looped her arm through Elsa's and guided her to the door. "You go pick those berries. I'll bring that picnic up later and we can all enjoy this beautiful day." On the porch Gita sat in a rocker and held two tiny gray kittens. She looked up and it was Elsa's face Evalyn saw, as if it was only a breath ago. Elsa on Morris Island yearning to learn from her teacher.

But so much had changed in three decades.

"Get the last of the berries," called Evalyn while watching Elsa meander on the upward path behind the cottage. "Maybe there will be enough for a pie! Gita, your Farfar will be ready in a moment."

Evalyn re-entered the home and walked to the rocker. She rested her hand on the pillow that concealed the paper. She sighed. The years and the distance and a new life had made the months spent on Morris Island seem like a brief scene in a literary novel. They had all shut that book and allowed it to collect dust on a back shelf.

Evalyn willed her hand to draw out the newspaper. She again unfolded it and stared at the headline. She sat in her rocker and began to read. She read some of the report and then skimmed the rest. Her eyes settled on the photograph of the lighthouse. A burning sensation irritated her throat and her chest tightened. She read the sidebar. Breath left her at the mention of Agnes' name.

"What's this? Where's Elsa? Gita?" asked Lias when he exited his bedroom clothed in his daily attire: flannel under canvas. Colder winter air would eventually require a heavy wool sweater between the layers.

"Elsa brought this … an Asheville newspaper. A report. The Charleston earthquake. Thirty years. Can you believe it's been 30 years?"

Lias looked down at her. She folded the newspaper and extended it to him.

"Yes," he said, slowly. "I know it's been 30 years. I spend extra time on my knees each year thankful that He made beauty from ashes, yes?" Lias took a deep breath and lingered his gaze on the hint of fall foliage just outside the window. "I don't read newspaper. No need."

"But Elsa thought that …"

"No need."

He kissed his wife on her forehead and stepped out to the porch.

"Gita! You come to climb the tower today?"

"Yes, Farfar!"

"Then let's go." Lias turned and winked at Evalyn.

From the porch, Evalyn watched Lias and their granddaughter, slender and long-legged, walk hand in hand to the barn where he kept two Rocky Mountain spotted mares. They could hike, but Gita loved to ride. Evalyn waited for them to saddle the horses and ride up the trail toward Wayah Bald before returning inside the cottage.

Evalyn looked once more at the Asheville newspaper, lingering for a few seconds on the photograph of the lighthouse. Her index finger touched lightly the tower where she had once stood and marveled that prisms of glass could save lives. She folded the paper neatly and tossed it onto the morning's smoldering embers. She remembered the light from the Charleston fire blazing far in the distance. She remembered the light, bright and steady, from the Fresnel lens.

It was time to burn the letter as well. She had held onto it for too long. But first she would crack open the past and allow it to remind her only once more what Agnes had given up so that she could have.

Evalyn went into her bedroom and retrieved the inlayed-oyster-shell cypress box from underneath her undergarments in the bottom drawer of their wardrobe. She laid it carefully on the bed, raised the lid, and lifted the small crinkled envelope. She unfolded the three yellowing pages; the first was in Lias' now-familiar bold script. She noted again the date. That her mother had died just one week prior to the letter's arrival always struck Evalyn as providential.

April 28, 1887

Dear Evalyn (Miss Gray),

Please come to us.

The children request it of you. I ask you. She wanted it.

Please read the enclosed letter so you will understand.

And then come to us.

Yours very sincerely, Lias (Mr. Larsson)

She pressed the short letter to her chest. The words, "Please come to us," touched her no matter how many times she read them or thought of them. She carefully refolded the single sheet of paper and returned it to the box.

The other two pages were written in Agnes' erratic hand; lines and lines of words in her native Swedish. Evalyn had never asked Lias, but the letter's English translation, written for her benefit, must have been for him an arduous and poignant undertaking.

To my husband, Lias,

I write this today because I can. My mind is not dark today. It is not light either. But I can see my way to write my thoughts.

This woman, who we call Miss Gray, has been a good teacher. You were right to employ her for our children. I did not want a teacher. You did. You were right. I cannot teach them. I hate her for teaching them, but I admire her as well. I hate it when the children smile at her or laugh. But I am happy inside when they do, as well. I watch them through the window as they leave for the beach and I am angry. But I do not want to go with them.

Inside my head there is the wind and it blows loud for a while and then softly, and I am fine and then I am not fine. So quickly I am not fine. So quickly.

And now when I am writing I feel the earth moving. It is moving me. But no one else feels it. It is moving me to the light. It is forcing me to the light. And when you are up in the light, and the children are sleeping and Miss Gray is sleeping, I look up to the spinning light – mostly when my head, my mind, is all dark – so very dark. I want to be up there with you and let the light flood out all this darkness. I want to be right for you, but I cannot be.

I think the light is looking for me sometimes. I think the earth is moving under me, telling me to go to the light. Go! Go! Go! One day soon, very soon, I think I will go.

You are a patient husband. You want a good wife with a good mind. I did not want to leave Sweden because I knew the darkness would follow me. I kept it hidden when I was on the farm, but the lighthouse light does not want the darkness to stay in the dark.

I know you care and you love, and I know you do want me to have a strong mind and to care and love as you do. But it will never be. Never be for me.

But she has a strong mind, and a strong heart. A good mind to teach children, always. A good heart, with no darkness, to love them. She can always teach them and care for them, as I cannot. And care for you. As I cannot.

You are faithful husband. I know. But I see how my darkness becomes yours.

Let her be what I cannot be. Call her to you when it is time.

I must go to the light. The earth will not stop moving until I let the light take my darkness.

Agnes did not sign the letter. She had ended it and folded it, and Lias had found it as she had intended him to.

After reading it once more, Evalyn placed the open letter on the remaining log of the small fire, newly fueled by the newspaper. She turned away and did not watch it burn.

She stopped in the middle of the room. Outside, the sun's rays illuminated leaves already tinged with gold. She allowed herself a moment of contemplation, remembering what Lias had shared with her during their first night together when she arrived in the mountains: "I will say this to you one time, and then I wish no more to speak of it. The night of the earthquake, I forgot to lock the door … I found her at the top … she reached out her hand for the light." Evalyn remembered him pausing, his words stifled. But he had swallowed and continued, slowly: "I tried to take her hand. She shook her head no. I begged her. When the Fresnel came around to meet her, she stumbled backwards and over the railing. I could not save her. She did not want to be saved.

And I did not understand why she did not want to be saved … until I found her letter."

Evalyn looked once more out the window. It was as bright and clear a day as any she could remember. She went back into the bedroom to return the box to the wardrobe. Lias would ask why it was out. Before she closed the lid, she shuffled items around – a few seashells, a clipping of sea oats, some handmade cards – until she found Samuel's few letters, tied together with rough twine. She held them for a moment and thought of Samuel. She did not need to re-read them. The knowledge contained in the correspondence, that Samuel had attended Wilberforce, met his wife there, married, fathered three children, and taught at a secondary school in his wife's native Ohio, after spending a year teaching on James Island, was all she needed to know. He had become a teacher; she knew he would. And once a year, usually at Christmas, he updated her on his life, always expressing his vision of integrated schools in South Carolina and all throughout the South.

She arranged her treasured items neatly in her father's handmade box so that it closed securely, and she tucked it in the wardrobe and covered it with undergarments.

She made her way to the larder. A bit of ham, some biscuits, apples, and boiled eggs were added to a cloth in a woven basket. Evalyn folded the cloth edges securely around the food.

She walked back to the woodstove, pulled aside the protective screen, and used a long metal rod to poke at the logs. No traces of the letter remained. The newspaper had also disappeared – except for a small sliver crouched in a corner, away from a tiny flame. She used the metal rod to draw the shred of paper closer to the woodstove door's opening. The image was of the top half of the Morris Island lighthouse. Evalyn stared at it for a moment and, with a stove shovel, scooped up the piece and placed it directly onto the flame. The newsprint flared brightly for only a second, and then it turned black.

Evalyn closed the woodstove's door and pulled the damper handle.

On the porch, Folly waited, ready, tail wagging. Evalyn pulled tight the laces securing her sturdy boots – men's boots, but it did not matter in the mountains. She looked up and up toward Wayah's peak. She left the cottage to ascend a path that would take her to her husband, her family, who waited for her in the fire tower.

ACKNOWLEDGEMENTS/AUTHOR'S NOTE

Thank you to the Charleston County Public Library for assisting me numerous times in gleaning newspaper articles, telegrams (like the one from Queen Victoria to President Grover Cleveland), and firsthand oral history accounts pertaining to the earthquake of August 31, 1886, which is still to-date the worst earthquake to affect the East Coast of the United States.

Thank you to former Folly Beach mayor Dr. Richard Beck, DDS, for inspiring me so many years ago while I was on assignment for *South Carolina* magazine; his mention of a teacher rowed out to teach the lighthouse keeper's children intrigued me and set ablaze this story.

Thank you to McLeod Plantation Historic Site for allowing me to tag along on so many excellent living history talks, and to just sit for hours under the great oaks heavy-laden with Spanish moss and absorb the sense of a place connoting both evil and beauty.

And, I am indebted to the great inspiration of Nathanial Hawthorne; his tedious *The Scarlet Letter* opening chapter, "The Custom House," in which he captivates the readers with his own experiences

and then fictionalized "discovery" of an embroidered letter "A,"
established the foundation for his great and classic novel, but it also
established the foundation for this novel. And, like Hawthorne's novel,
Light Fracture is mostly historically accurate, but a woman named Agnes
Larsson did not fall to her death at the Morris Island lighthouse. Her
story and that of the character Evalyn Gray is fictitious. However,
goings on at the lighthouse in the 19th century and some of the names
of actual keepers; earthquake damage to the lighthouse; and, the overall
history of the lighthouse is all historically accurate. Details in the
prologue and throughout the novel about the Civil War,
Reconstruction, and the earthquake are accurate. Plus, the textbooks
that teachers were referencing and using at the time – as well as texts
that Evalyn read regarding mental illness are accurate as well.

 I would also be remiss if I did not express my admiration of
Southern literary great Pat Conroy, who provided thrilling
encouragement of my work to a Charleston Library Society crowd just
months before he passed in 2016. Pat championed the work of
Southern writers and he is sorely missed. And, my admiration of early
20th century novelist Edith Wharton is what drew me to writing stories
in the first place. She wrote in her autobiography that she walked

around with her characters and lived with them for a while before she gave them life on pages. For this story, I have done just that for more than 15 years; Evalyn, Lias, Agnes, Elsa, and Erik are real to me, as is the activity in the house that was once next to the Morris Island lighthouse. In my imagination, it is a home I have occupied many times.

Finally, I am thankful for the opportunity to truly know Charleston, James Island, and Folly Beach, S.C., places forever steeped in the persistence of a bygone culture. So much time spent in these places is due to the generosity and hospitality of my sister, Meta, and her wonderful husband, Tim.

I soaked it all in – and now you have done the same through the reading of this novel.

ABOUT THE AUTHOR

Deena C. Bouknight, who resides in the Carolinas, is a career writer, having contributed for 30-plus years to local, regional, national, and international publications. Her two other Southern literary fiction works are *Broken Shells* and *Playing Guy*. And, she has contributed to *Portraits of Grace: North Carolina Churches* (Our State Books); *Humor for a Sister's Heart* (Howard); and, *Big Book of Christmas Joy* (Howard). Email Deena at dknight865@gmail.com.

Made in the USA
Middletown, DE
10 June 2021

41701690R00196